God Is a
Woman

Michael Tavon

CONTENTS

Acknowledgements.................................4

She Was Golden.................................5

Women.................................25

God Hates Me.................................49

Well, Isn't This Awkward.................................70

The Less I Feel, the Better.................................77

Happy Birthday, Iris.................................90

Runnin' on Empty.................................100

Joy to the World.................................108

Merry Fucking Christmas.................................119

The Visit to the Abortion Clinic.................................125

The Flight.................................136

Nine Months Later.................................138

ACKNOWLEDGMENTS

God, mother, father, and my two sisters.

She Was Golden

There I was sitting at the edge of the bar alone, sipping on the third glass of gin 'til I could taste the last half-melted ice cube through the straw, with suicidal thoughts dashing through my brain. At twenty-five years young, I was alone, poor, and had a dream that seemed impossible to achieve. I managed to alienate myself from old friends and loved ones. I was broken, and I wasn't seeking to be fixed.

It was Friday night, and everyone was dressed in their best attire, happily intoxicated with their friends or significant others. Some people were celebrating: love, success, or simply appreciating life, while I was wallowing in self-pity because I'd released my third novel and had barely sold one hundred and five copies. Fifteen more than my second title, and sixty more than my first.

Optimistically speaking, I was on my audience was growing. However, realistically speaking, I was a fucking failure. After all the sleepless nights, relentless promoting, blogging, and stress, I had only sold two hundred and twenty-five books.

Prior to the releasing of the title, my Facebook friends, Twitter followers, and real-life associates were so engaged and supportive. I projected to sell at least one thousand copies. Unfortunately, once the book hit the stores and websites, people stopped caring. The retweets, likes, and even the text messages were gone. It was like I'd died or worst, like, I'd never existed.

In Saint Petersburg, Florida people pretend to care and show half-assed support, but become diehard fans once you make it. Moreover, I have the worst luck with women, hence why I'm alone and half plastered on a Friday night.

I raise my head from staring into my empty glass and signaled to the bartender. "Lala, another one, please." I blurted out.

"Okay, but I'm closing your tab after this one, love," she responded.

"Why? I'm not driving," I told her.

"I don't want you to get so drunk to where you can't even call an Uber," she said.

"Uber? I thought I was leaving with you." I reached for her.

"Not tonight, baby." She shrugged and gave me a soft smile to soften the blow.

I noticed the cherry lipstick smudged over her front teeth. I wanted to say something, but didn't, and chuckled to myself instead.

She placed the drink in front of me. I took a huge swallow, then another, then another, and another. I winced as the alcohol slowly burned my insides. It was the type of pain that brought pleasure. I nearly choked as a chunk of ice slowly slid down my throat. Lala stood and watched to see if I was well enough to carry myself out

"Alright love, it's time to wrap it up," she said.

"I got a few rounds left in me," I said.

"No one knows your limit better than me, and I say you're done for tonight." She slid the bill towards me.

"Whatever you say," I slurred and her a fifty-dollar bill. Even though my funds were low, my pride wouldn't allow me to ask for change. "Keep the tip."

"Thanks. See you later, baby." She turned to the next customer.

I didn't want to waste any more time, so I chugged my drink so quickly I almost choked on my saliva. I slammed the empty glass on the bar and surveyed the area. My legs were still under me, but the ground made it feel like I was standing on a moon bounce. I bumped and nudged a couple of bar-goers as I made way to the exit.

"Watch your step, your putz," a scrawny gentleman yelled.

"Nice burn, Fonzie," I insulted and continued towards the exit.

A dainty palm gently landed on my chest as I reached for the door. The young woman appeared from a crowd standing nearby.

"Hey you're Price, Price Jones," she said. I flashed a wide smile when her exotic eyes met mine. "You're much taller than I expected," she added.

"Well, you know, I grew." I shrugged.

She stood about 5 feet 2, with rich brown skin, and short wavy hair. Her petite frame was complemented with salacious curves. She appeared to have no signs of stress, disappointment, or hardship.

"And y-yo-you are?" I stammered.

"Be-"

"Beautiful?" I interrupted. "Did I guess correctly?" It was a cheesy line I quickly regretted.

"No, silly." Her eyes rolled. "It's Benu." She nudged into me. She had such a piercing stare; the type that could see right through your soul. It was as if she was unaware of how beautiful she was. Within five minutes my heart was kicking in overdrive. I couldn't tell if it was the booze or if she was causing the adrenaline rush, but alcohol had never made me feel so good before.

"Oh, the Egyptian bird," I said. "I like." I winked. Her lips curled into the cutest smirk.

"You can call me Bee, though," she responded. She jumped and exclaimed, "I love this song!"

"Me too. But it's kind of weird they're playing it right now," I responded.

She leaned in closer to me. "Why so?" she asked.

"Don't get me wrong 'Every Breath You Take' is a beautiful song, but it's the last song I wanna hear when I'm getting hammered," I said.

She chuckled and placed her hand in mine. "You're funny. Come meet my friends."

I trailed her as we approached her friends who were a few feet away. A few moments prior I felt like I was walking upside down, but she made me feel sober. Nothing sobers me up quicker than a pretty face. I never wanted to be the guy who vomited on himself in front of a beautiful woman. So, I always remained the 'perfect drunk.'

"Hey guys, meet Price," she said. I waved. "He's the writer I've been telling you guys about."

"Nice to freaking meet ya." Her male friend pointed at me. "I'm Cam," he said. I reached for a handshake as he extended his arm for a fist bump. After three failed attempts, our hands finally connected on a proper handshake. I quickly withdrew from his warm clammy palm.

"Nice to meet you, too." I wiped my hand on the hip of my pants.

Cam was a few inches taller than me. He wore a fishnet shirt and close-fitting blue jeans that would have made Patrick Swayze proud. His hair was styled in a messy-greasy aesthetic. We converse

9

about sports and movies; we both liked the Lakers and the Cowboys as well as anything Will Farrell. Their other friend interrupted to introduce herself. She was frail and pale.

"Hey, I'm Melanie. Call me Mel." She smiled, exposing her oddly spaced teeth. I leaned in for a hug, and she embraced me back. My nose twitched when I caught a whiff of her putrid body odor. She reeked of something awful. She was a chipper woman and seemed like the type to get high off life.

"So, you like Queen, huh?" I nodded at her shirt.

"Who?"

"Queen, the band, on your shirt."

"Oh, I don't know any of their songs, to be honest." She laughed. "It's a killer shirt, though."

I shook my head. Nothing screams pretentious more than wearing the shirt of a band you have no knowledge of. I turned to Benu, jealousy struck when I saw her entertaining another guy a few feet away. By the look on his face, the conversation was going well. Her slender body was nothing short of perfect in a tight red dress. I began to imagine the things I wanted to do to her.

Melanie was speaking to me, but nothing was heard. Banu's smile from a distance had me in a trance.

Damn, beauty like this doesn't come every day, I thought.

Cam wrapped his arm around my shoulder and clenched tightly. I tried to escape from his hold, but his grip was too strong.

"Isn't Kevin Hart's new movie awesome? He's the funniest," he said.

"Nah. He's not funny to me."

"You're right. He can be corny at times, and overrated too."

I raised my upper lip and shook my head. I tugged my shoulder, and he finally released his grasp. He offered me a sip of his drink, but I waved my finger. I was never the one to reject a free drink, but I was beginning to feel uncomfortable around him. Either his eye kept twitching or he was winking at me. I couldn't tell.

"You straight?" I asked.

"The hell kinda is question is that?" he asked. "I love vagina."

"No, idiot. I meant, straight as in are you okay? Your eye keeps twitching."

"No, it's not." His eyes twitched again.

"There it is." I pointed. "You did it again."

"Dude, you're drunk." He took a sip of his drink and turned to Melanie.

Benu tugged my sleeve. We locked eyes again this time the connection was longer. She bit her bottom lip. I took her by the wrist and opened the door. We left her friends behind, but they didn't even notice because they were already making out.

We strolled the strip and talked about a little of everything. She mostly boasted about my writing. I'd never met a person who was so infatuated with my work. She recited lines of my poetry and her favorite quotes from my stories. The feeling of being admired felt new all over again. She made me believe people were out there watching. Her eyes had me drawn to her. She seemed nothing like her friends. They were nice people, but she was magnetic.

"How did you meet those two?" I asked.

"I met Mel at LA Fitness and Cam is her on again off again boyfriend, but not boyfriend."

"You mean a situationship?"

She nodded. "Yeah. I hate those. Why are people so afraid to commit these days? People pretend to be in relationships. It's pathetic." She said with passion.

I wrapped my arm around her shoulder. "Because some people are tired of getting hurt, so they keep their emotions bottled in and screw each other's brains out."

"That's not healthy."

"It's less painful than love."

"Hey, I wanna dance. Let's go to Push." She jumped as we walked past the club. I was relieved she'd changed the topic. I didn't want to get in one of my melancholy moods and turn her off. I often tended to self-indulge in my own sadness.

12

"Where they play crappy house music? Nah, I'm good." I declined.

"C'mon. Don't be such a loser." She tugged my arm. "I'll pay your way."

"Let's go."

"Well, giddy up." She hopped on my back and I carried us three venues down and waited for entry. I hated clubs with a passion, black clubs especially: long lines, expensive watered-down drinks, the disc jockey played the same songs all night, and the people were snobby stiffs. My generation no longer lived for the moment. People couldn't take a piss without snapping a picture of themselves.

But she made me feel alive. That night, I would have climbed a mountain with her. Her energy was infectious.

The club was packed with drugged-out white people dancing off-beat to irritating EDM renditions of rap songs, and Flo-Rida's music (I hate Flo-Rida). That's one thing I love about Caucasians, they don't care who's watching or where they are, they're going to dance without a care in the world. The music blasted at a tone-deafening volume. I lead Benu to the dance floor. She began jumping and fist pumping. I couldn't help but laugh.

"Don't stand there and be a boob. Have some fun." She grabbed my shirt.

For the first time in my life, I decided to let go and become uninhibited. We raved together like two carefree souls. We swallowed shots of Fireball and

13

danced like we were the only two there. When it approached two thirty in the morning, she invited me to her place a few blocks away. Her legs were tired from walking in heels all night, so we caught a cab.

During the ride, she told me about herself. She was from Southside Chicago. Dirty literature was a guilty pleasure. An animal enthusiast. A brain cancer survivor and she'd moved to Florida to escape the toxic environment of her home.

When we arrived at her apartment complex, I hugged her and bid her goodnight. I remained in the cab as she exited.

"What are you doing?" she asked.

"Huh?"

"You're such a dork. Come on up," she said. I crawled out the backseat.

Her elevator was out of service and her unit was on the seventh floor. I carried her the first two flights of stairs. She walked the next two flights. I carried her the rest of the way. She was lightweight, but the temperature of the stairwell was warm and dry. By the time we made it to her door, I had my hands on my hips while gasping for air and my sweater was soaked with sweat.

"You're such a wimp." She laughed. I was too gassed to make a quip. I loved a woman with sass and Benu had plenty of it.

When we entered her apartment, she politely told me to take my dirty Vans off. I stood in the living room as she walked to her bedroom. She

14

quickly came back with a washcloth and towel then escorted me to the bathroom.

I took a long shower. I stood under the huge square showerhead and let the warm water stream through my hair and to my body. I felt purified and relaxed. She came knocking on the door because I had the water running for too long. I dried off and put my dirty boxers back on. My throat was sore, so I raided her medicine cabinet. There were three half empty medicine bottles meticulously placed in the far-left corner; one on each row, with the labels facing the wall. I ogled those bottles as if one of them contained the cure for cancer. She knocked on the door again.

"Is everything okay?" she asked through the door.

"I'll be out in a minute."

I splashed some water on my face and left the bathroom. I noticed the creative décor as I walked the hallway leading to her bedroom. Her walls were a warm purple with eclectic paintings. There was a painting of an Empress ruling a colony of men.

I always believed a woman could rule the world and it was nice to finally meet one who believed it too.

Her bedroom door was cracked. The scent of cinnamon tickled my nose when I entered. Persian rugs covered the floor and chill wave music played through the speakers. She sat Indian style on her bed reading Portions from a Wine-Stained Notebook by Charles Bukowski. A bong-shaped lamp, placed on top of her nightstand, provided dim lighting. She wore pink boy shorts, a long white tank top, and

15

wide black frames over her small face. I smiled and said, "Wonderful place you have here."

"Thanks. Are you gonna stand there or join me?"

I plunged on top of her bed like an Olympic diver. The mattress wobbled, and she tilted to the side.

"Nice water bed too," I said. She giggled. I hadn't seen a waterbed since my mother had one when I was a toddler.

After the water had settled, I placed my head on her lap. She continued to read the book while rubbing my beard. I grinned and looked at her.

"I love how you smile with your eyes, and you have beautiful teeth too." She winked. I sat next to her.

"Thank you." I smiled. We locked eyes again. I went in to kiss her. She was too timid to meet me halfway, so I stopped.

"You're one handsome son of a bitch."

"What?" I raised a brow.

"You heard me." She puckered her lips and sized me up.

"And for what it's worth, this has been the best night in a long time for me."

"I'm glad I was able to help," she said. "Flip over."

"What are you gonna do to me?" I asked.

"Do it."

16

She pinched my chest, so I flipped over. She straddled my back. Her soft fingers caressed my neck, shoulders and lower back. I sighed a breath of relief. She leaned in and whispered,

"I'm a masseuse," then kissed the side of my neck.

"And I'm in love," I said with my face planted in her pillow.

"What?"

"This feels great," I said through her pillow.

"I bet."

She lathered my back with lotion and stroked me with her warm hands. I drifted into a dream as she rubbed my back and planted her soft lips on my neck. I was too drunk to wake up and too paranoid to have sex. I knew she wanted it, but I didn't have a condom. Usually I would 'roll the dice,' but those medicine bottles had given me the goose bumps. I remained stretched across her bed with my eyes shut tight.

That night was the best sleep I'd had in years. The water mattress made it feel like I was resting on a cloud. I cuddled her petite body, and her scent was so sweet. I had the whole wide world in my arms. That's how she made me feel.

The next morning, I was awakened by the cadence of my throbbing headache. A small steaming cup of tea rested on the nightstand. I took a few sips, finding it to be lightly sweet and minty. She entered the room. Her hair was in a messy bun and she wore

17

black panties and a white Fleetwood Mac shirt covered in droplets of paint. Her waist was still partially moist. She handed me a plate of French toast, turkey sausage, and egg whites.

"Thanks, beautiful," I said, grabbing the plate.

"You're welcome."

"Those paintings on the wall, are those yours?"

"Yes." She nodded. "It's something I do on the side."

"You're freaking awesome."

"Thank you." She smiled. "Eat up. I hope you enjoyed the tea." She winked and swished her hips as she walked away.

I took my time eating. I wanted to savor it. After I had finished, I took the dirty dishes to the kitchen and washed them myself. She was in the living room working on a new piece.

I sat next to her and watched as she stroked the canvas with her paintbrush. We talked about time travel, spaceships, and our favorite moments from *The Office*. After she had finished painting, she drove me home.

My home was only a twelve-minute drive from downtown, but the environments were like heaven and hell. My neighborhood looked hopeless; filled with abandoned houses, and brown lawns. My house was an old-aged two-story unit. The overhanging roof was caved in from heavy rain storms.

I kissed her cheek and exited the car.

"I'll call you," I said.

"You better." She smirked.

I gazed off into the distance as she drove away. I stood with my chest out and a confident smirk on my face. I was content yet slightly saddened as I lost sight of her red Prius, only because I didn't want our moment to end. I barely knew her, but when you meet someone special, you know.

I stood in the driveway for a few minutes, thinking about her. I couldn't wait to see her again. I strutted to the front door feeling like a new man.

When I entered the house a large cloud of smoke floated towards my face. I rushed to the stove to remove a burning pot of rice. My lungs collapsed. I ran outside for a few minutes to catch my breath. I sprinted back in and opened all the doors and windows.

"Mom? Jay? Ash?" I shouted.

A loud thud erupted from my mother's room, so I rushed upstairs.

"Mom," I yelled as I ran into her room.

She laid on the floor trembling, curled in the fetal position next to an empty syringe. Her cold skin sent chills through my palms. I positioned her to the side to prevent her from choking on her own vomit.

19

Clunks of her blond hair fell into my sweaty palm. My upper lip began to quiver. I dialed 911.

"911 operator. What is your emergency?"

"My mother overdosed. Please send help. She's dying."

I provided her name, address and all the other irrelevant information the operator asked of me. I see why so many people die before an ambulance arrives. Getting some help shouldn't require so many questions and answers.

"She's white, by the way," I added.

"No, worries," the operator responded. "Someone will be there soon."

I had mentioned her race to create a sense of urgency. The last time an ambulance had been called to this neighborhood the victim had already drowned in his own blood before they arrived. It took them forty minutes to drive two miles. Traffic must have been heavy at 12:45 am.

He was a good kid; seventeen years young, honor roll student, and tri-sport all American. Allen Ross was his name. His house got raided and he'd attempted to protect his family. He'd suffered three gunshots to the chest. The killer was a fellow teammate who'd had no clue Allen resided there.

I tilted my mother's head, lifted her chin, and pinched her nose. I sealed her lips with my shaking fingers and huffed two quick breaths into her mouth. I repeated the process every two minutes.

"Everything's gonna be fine." I kissed her forehead.

A cop car and ambulance arrived twelve minutes later. I guess mentioning her race helped after all.

I stayed home to wait for my siblings to arrive. I didn't want to alarm them. They're too young to be worried about our mother's well-being. Jordan, the seventeen-year-old 'dark' child of the trio. He identifies himself as pansexual. I never understood the definition of it, but our family coined it as a phase and never paid much attention to it. He's a bright kid nonetheless. My eight-year-old sister, Ashlyn, suffers with mild autism, because our mother was shooting up while pregnant.

Growing up as the only child of color in our family was traumatic, to say the least. I had been abused by their father, Thomas: mentally, physically and sexually. He was short and stocky with spotted skin from his lasting sunburns.

I often found myself waking up in cold sweats from vivid nightmares of him fondling me with his grimy hands while I was asleep. He made me feel worthless and unwanted. Every time I saw his smug face the burning passion to impale a knife through his kidney arrived. I had been too embarrassed to tell anyone what had been happening.

One day, Thomas packed his bags, drove to West Palm Beach and never looked back. We hadn't heard from him since.

A few hours later Jordan arrived. He was dead silent as he walked through the door with his slouched posture. I snatched the orange tinted shades off his face.

"Another fresh one, eh, Jay?" I held his chin.

Jordan shook his head and dragged his feet across the floor. Jordan's eye was swollen shut and his shirt was ripped. He had the strength of an ox; nothing could break him. I don't know how he managed to maintain his sanity while being tortured every day at school, in the neighborhood, and via social media. Attending a predominately black school made things even worse.

Ashlyn got dropped off by her bus driver shortly after. She was my heart, so pure and harmless and it was my job to keep her that way. Neither Jordan nor Ashlyn asked of mother's whereabouts. They assumed she was somewhere shooting up. They'd grown accustomed to sleeping without their mother at home.

I decided to go back to Benu's house. We smoked weed, painted, and cuddled on her couch as we watched *How I Met Your Mother* on Netflix. I'd always loved that show because of Ted. He was such a hopeful romantic and it was pathetic. I knew what it was like to have such high hopes for a woman, just to get disappointed.

The night was going well until Benu's demeanor changed. She suddenly became standoffish. She wouldn't look at me and refused to let me touch her. She treated me like a stranger.

"Excuse you. What the hell are you doing?" she said snapped when I rubbed her thigh.

"I was just..."

"Trying to fuck?" She sat upright and snatched the blanket off me. I hopped up.

"No," I said quickly.

"You're like every other asshole I've ever met. Get the fuck out," she hissed. "Chill out. It's not serious."

"Get out!" she yelled.

"Well, I would love to stay, but you're a crazy bitch," I retorted, hurt by her sudden change of demeanor. I got dressed and stormed out without closing the door.

I took a long hike along the biking trail. I lit a smoke and sucked on the butt. The sky was dark and plain, no clouds, no stars, just the wide moon staring down at me. As I continued to plod and smoke, I saw a woman cradling her toddler son, while resting on the grass. She had a grocery cart filled with torn blankets and a jug of water. I walked over and gave her ten dollars. She held my hand firmly and put it to her forehead.

"God bless you," she said. I nodded and walked away.

My hamstrings were beginning to stiffen, so I lit another cigarette. The route home seemed to get longer and darker the further I walked. Every time a smoke went out I sparked another. My fingertips caught a burn by the fifth cancer stick. I grimaced at the sting.

When I got home, I grabbed the bottle of bourbon and stood on the patio. I took swig after swig until I was numb inside. Numbness was the closest feeling to being dead, and I loved it. People never understood my pain. Neither did I, but I knew I hated myself and wanted no parts of what I saw in the mirror every morning.

I thought about Benu. I hoped to get back in her good graces soon. She was the first woman to put a smile on my face in a long time, and I needed to smile more often. I didn't want to lose her so quickly. I deserved a second chance. I needed a second chance.

WOMEN

Two weeks had past and Benu still hadn't tried to call or text me. I figured she was done, wanted no parts of me or had found another guy. I still saw the perfection in her, and I hoped she saw the good in me. Women were my kryptonite and I had fallen weak for them on numerous occasions. I admired everything about them; their grace, their touch; their love; and their inspiration. Unfortunately, women also had a way of making me feel cheap.

I was eating Cinnamon Toast Crunch and watching SpongeBob with Ashlyn when I noticed Jordan rapidly pacing through the house as if he had too many things on his mind. He grabbed his keys, fixed a sandwich, put on his shoes, and poured a glass of water. He stopped to watch TV for a moment then put on a faded black Pearl Jam shirt. I laughed.

"Going on a date or something?" I asked.

"To a friend's house." He laughed and rushed out the door. He was in a lively mood. It was nice to see him smile for a change.

Ashlyn and I continued to watch Squidward get tangled in SpongeBob and Patrick's shenanigans for a few hours until we were interrupted by heavy knocks on the door. I assumed they were coming from a bill collector or a drug dealer, so I ignored them. The knocks grew louder and more aggressive. I rushed to the door, but peeped out the window before opening it. Benu stood outside with aviator shades covering her eyes and wearing blue jeans and a white tee shirt.

"You're dressed like a lesbian from the late 80s," I said as I swung the door open.

"Thank you." She smiled and invited herself in. She kicked her shoes off and began to tour the house. "Lovely place, quaint but nice," she said.

"Thanks. I try to keep it safe, clean, and simple for my sister."

Ashlyn was tapping her forehead with the remote repetitively. A look of empathy dawned on Benu's face as she gazed at my sister. She could tell something was wrong with Ashlyn because of her spacy glare.

"Is she okay?" she asked.

"She's autistic."

She gasped. "I'm sorry."

26

"It's cool. Come sit with us," I said. She smiled, but sat on the furthest side of the couch leaving me space to sit between them. I offered her water and snacks, but she rejected every suggestion. I got a bit offended because practicing hospitality was something I never did. An hour later Benu, Ashlyn and I were still watching SpongeBob.

I wrapped my arm around Benu. She hesitated to lean her head on my shoulder. Ashlyn began to growl and tug my sleeve. "Calm down, sis. It's okay," I whispered to her.

"What?" Benu asked.

"Nothing." Ashlyn clamored for my attention. I wrapped my other arm around her. "How about some bourbon?" I asked.

She started to say no, but the stern look on my face gave her a sudden change of heart.

"Did you say bourbon?"

"Yes, follow me into the kitchen." We stood. "I'll be right back, okay?" I told Ashlyn and planted a kiss on her forehead.

I took Benu by the hand and strolled to the kitchen, two feet away.

For a two-story house, the bottom half was congested. The kitchen, living room, sitting room, and bathroom were all short distances away from each other. Even the entrance to my room was nearby. I had turned the garage into my personal cold dark man cave. For numerous nights I entrapped myself and indulged in alcohol and painkillers until I was comfortably numb, in peace.

Once we stepped into the kitchen I grabbed two glasses and filled them with ice and whiskey.

We took sips from our glasses. There was a silence among us. I wasn't going to say anything. I was waiting for her to crack. I cleared my throat to create some noise. The only racket amid us was Ashlyn's obnoxious laughter.

"You wanna come to my room?" I asked. She nodded. I waved to Ashlyn as we walked to my room. I pushed the door open.

"Wow your man cave is clean," Benu said.

"Smells good too," I grinned.

She gulped the remains of her drink then stretched across my bed. "

Your room is so cold," she said as she wrapped herself in my blanket.

"Just like my heart," I sipped from my glass.

"I love these comics, too. Gosh, it showcases your inner child," she said gazing at my walls.

"It started when I was twelve, my obsession I mean," I said.

"How so?"

I sat on the edge of my bed and poured another glass of bourbon.

"Every time my father got released from prison he would visit me," I took another sip. "And when he did, he gave me four, five, six comic books, and I would take those pictures and tape them to my wall."

"Cool." She smiled.

"As you can see, he went to jail a lot."

Her mouth turned crooked as she held back the laughter. "I'm sorry," she said.

"It's okay. I laugh about it all the time," I responded and laid next to her.

We cuddled for a few minutes. She started to poke her ass out more and more. I was reluctant to make a move because of what had happened before, but my dick got aroused.

"I'm sorry," she said through her teeth. I raised my brow.

29

"Huh?"

"For what I did the other day," she said. "You're such an amazing guy, and I didn't want to be another quick fuck, so I blacked out."

"No worries," I whispered in her ear. "It won't be quick." I kissed her cheek.

"Get off me, you jerk." She laughed and wiggled her shoulders. I pulled her to me. She turned over on her back, and I rubbed her clit through her jeans. Her eyes rolled, and she let out the softest moan. I pulled the blanket off her body and stripped her of her clothes while kicking my pants and boxers off. I positioned myself between her legs. I stroked until every inch of me was inside of her. For a tiny woman, she could take good deep stroking. She made my eyes roll. She was so warm and so wet. Five minutes felt like an eternity.

"Hey Price, can we-" Jordan started to ask, as the door swung open and stood there with Ashlyn by his side. Their drop and eyes widen at what they'd witnessed. I looked at Benu.

Her eyes were shut tight and her lips were sunken inwards.

Ashlyn screamed loud enough to crack a window. Jordan covered her eyes with his hands.

"Bro, close the damn door," I yelled. He gave a thumb up and left the room.

Benu was shaking I couldn't tell if was out of shame or because of the coldness of my room. She got dressed, gave me a kiss and left out the back door.

I grinned cheek to cheek as I laid in the nude. I knew she was the one. After I had alleviated myself of the blue balls, I went to the living room to see what the kids were doing. Jordan was reading off his Kindle notepad, and Ashlyn was scribbling in her coloring book. They seemed to be unbothered by what they'd seen.

"Your girlfriend's pretty," Ashlyn said.

"Thanks, sis." I hugged her.

"And how was your day, Jay?" I asked

"The same as yours." He winked. My heart was filled with joy and excitement. I felt like a proud father.

"Who's the lucky

person?" "Aileen."

I was pleased knowing Jordan had lost his virginity to a woman. Even though I had no problems with his sexuality, I wanted him to

31

feel the magic of a woman before exploring other territories.

Later that evening, I went to Bayfront Hospital, where my mother was fighting for her life. I've always said if you don't die between waiting for the ambulance and during the ambulance ride, you will most likely die in the bed. This hospital sucks. The doctors are lazy. The food tastes like gourmet prison dishes, and it's filthy. I once came in for a routine check-up and left with an ear infection. Unfortunately, it's the closest hospital to us.

Luckily, her room was on the third floor, so I didn't have to wait for those wretched elevators. I took the stairs instead. When I entered her room, there were three doctors. I hoped they were like Dr. House and his crew, but I knew it was only wishful thinking.

One assistant reclined on the sofa chair reading a Jet magazine, and the other flipped through channels on the television.

"Hey, Mr. Jones. I'm sorry no visitors at this hour." Dr. Keller approached me.

"Fuck off." I nudged him. "What the fuck y'all been doing this whole time?" I yelled as I looked at my mother's body.

Her skin had turned a light shade of purple, and she was drifting in and out of consciousness. I visited her regularly, but I never brought the kids along. I knew she was dying and there was nothing I could do about it. I didn't want her children to see their mother fighting to take her final breaths.

The lead surgeon, Dr. Henry, walked into the room dragging his long feet across the scuffed floor. He would usually tread in with a dopey look in his eyes and his eyebrows reaching for the top of his forehead, or he would have a light smile on his face. This time his face was dull and straightforward, and his skinny broad shoulders were hunched. I knew something was wrong. He shook my hand and stared me dead in the eyes. My bottom lip began to tremble as I prepared myself for the news.

"We tried everything. She has no more than a week left."

"What's wrong with her?"

I lost control of my head as it wandered from left to right, right to left, up and down, down and up. I couldn't look him in the eye. The ground seemed to have shifted, because my legs were trembling.

"Her kidneys, lungs, and heart are

shot." "Y'all couldn't find a donor?"

"Not this fast, especially for someone who doesn't have insurance."

"'Bullshit."

"Sir." He placed his palm on my chest.

"Get the fuck off me." I swatted his hand. "Y'all don't want to save her 'cause she's a junkie, huh?"

"Not the case. We have a long waiting list and it may take months to find a match."

"What about me?"

He gave a grin of empathy. "Son, she's gone."

I swallowed the huge lump in my throat as I came to the realization of my mother's demise. I knew her legacy or lack thereof was dwindling, and the memories of her would slowly fade until she became an empty, forgotten soul.

Most of us become forgotten long before we die, which makes being alive pointless at times.

Even as her child I couldn't recollect any fond memories of her. Instead, I remembered missed birthdays, never having a Christmas tree, no family vacations. But I loved her wholeheartedly.

My face turned to stone as I peered at her soon to be paling corpse. I wanted to cry, but I couldn't. My heart refused to let me cry for a stranger. I'd saved her life on many occasions. I guess, subconsciously, I was relieved. Her struggle was over and now her spirit could finally live in solidarity.

"Okay," I said. I cleared my throat and rushed out the door.

I took an Uber back home. Sade was playing through the radio which made me feel better.

"By the look in your eyes I can tell you didn't receive good news," the driver said.

"True," I managed to croak out.

"I'm sorry. This ride is on me," he said.

"Thank you."

The driver remained silent during the duration of the ride. It was so irritating when Uber drivers asked twenty-one questions as if they cared about what's going on in my life. I loved it when they just shut up and drove.

Half of the sky was filled with gray clouds; the other side was ocean blue. The atmosphere was dry and humid as usual. My mother's favorite song 'I Wanna Dance' by Whitney Houston, begun to play through the speakers. I smiled as I remembered her dancing along to Whitney's voice as she cooked breakfast. She used to make: French toast, bacon, grits with shrimp, every Saturday morning when I was a child.

Suddenly the vehicle came to an abrupt halt. My forehead bumped against the back of the headrest.

"Dude, what the hell?" I exclaimed, rubbing my forehead. He turned his head.

"Sorry. There was a squirrel in the road. Are you okay?" He glanced at me.

"You almost got me hurt over a fucking squirrel?" I asked in bewilderment.

"Sorry, bro."

"Yo, drop me off here."

He pulled over on the side of the road, and I rushed out the vehicle. Since he'd been nice giving me a free ride, I kept my negative comments to myself and closed the door behind me and walked away.

I stopped at the gas station on the corner and grabbed a twelve pack of Budweiser and a pack of swishers. I arrived home a few minutes later. A black BMW was parked outside. Our lawn was overgrown and filled with crumpled brown paper bags and piles of dog shit. But the unkempt grass was the least of my worries.

When I entered the house, Ashlyn was sitting on Iris's lap. She was reading poetry from my collection to her.

Whose Iris, you ask? She's the woman who broke my heart when I was twenty-one. My passion fell deep for her. I'd done everything I could to make her mine, and she'd led me on. I'd fallen for those deep brown eyes, curly afro, and her petite frame. And she was comfortable in her skin. Never wore makeup or fake weave. I loved when a woman could embrace her natural state because that's how God created her.

Everything was going well until one night she'd came over and told me she was pregnant. The baby wasn't mine obviously because we'd never fucked. Instead, she was screwing local rapper named Young Crack. I had become depressed for weeks. Deceit has a way of making a person feel belittled and stupid.

It's strange how some women hold out on sex with the man who cares about them, but open their legs for the men who have no intentions on falling in love with them.

She'd gotten an abortion, and we'd tried to get over it, but things got intense between us.

Each argument led to the abortion being mentioned. The thought of her conceiving someone else's child ate me alive. With that dark cloud looming over us, we'd gone our separate ways. She'd moved to Fort Lauderdale to accept a job for the school board.

For three years we'd kept in touch sporadically. She would come home to visit her family once in a blue moon. She would come by and we'd get high and forget the bullshit we'd gone through. Once we'd come down, our issues came back to haunt us.

Somehow, she'd managed to keep a small space in my heart and she knew it. Iris always made sure to lure me back in whenever she felt my presence fading away. Even when my love belonged to someone else, she found a way to come back.

"It's been a while, Mr. Jones," Iris said.

"Hey, Ash," I greeted. Ashlyn waved.

"Are you ignoring me?" Iris asked.

"I'm kind of busy, so I'll go to my room now." I proceeded to reach for the door handle.

"I'll be in there soon," she shouted.

"Don't come in unless you're naked," I said as I opened my bedroom door.

"Deal." She laughed. I slammed the door.

I took a bottle out of the box and twisted the cap off. I guzzled half of the beer and placed it on my dresser. I set the box of beer next to my bed. I took my sweater off and slumped on my bed. The door cracked opened. Iris peeked her head inside. She giggled. "It smells like vag," She covered her nose.

"The most wonderful aroma in the world," I said.

She sat at the edge of the bed. We locked eyes, until I shut mine tight. I didn't want to fall for her gaze. I grabbed another bottle. Beer spilled over my bedspread when I popped the cap. I took a few swigs.
She sat in silence letting her eyes wander.

"So, how's your mother?" she asked.

"She's dead." My eyes met hers.

"Not funny, Price." She covered her mouth.

"I know. That's why I told you."

"You're serious." Her jaw dropped.

I nodded. I sat upright and continued to drink from the bottle.

"What happened?" Her eyes began to tear up.

I cleared my throat. "She overdosed." She rubbed my back and wrapped her arm around my shoulder. I rested my head on her chest. She caressed my beard. She knew how much I loved when her soft fingers brushed against my scruff. I closed my eyes, and for a moment, everything was fine. As she stroked my face something gently grazed my skin. I grabbed her hand and there it was, a golden wedding band with mini diamonds along the ring. My chest felt like it had been stomped on by an elephant.

"You're engaged?"

"You didn't know? It's all over Facebook and Instagram," she said.

I gave her a cold blank stare. I had stopped using social media long ago. It was pointless. It's millions of people ranting nonsense about their personal lives and celebrities.

She inched closer to me. She attempted to touch my shoulder, but I lurched it back. Seeing her again brought back a bitter taste. A sting that was not yet healed.

"Why are you even here?" I stood.

"To see you. You don't call, text, or nothing. It's like I don't exist to you anymore."

"Because you don't."

"What?"

"We aren't friends, pen pals, nothing. Leave me alone."

"But Price."

"Leave." I gestured at the door. She wiped the tears from her eyes then walked towards the door. She stopped and looked over her shoulder. We locked eyes for a few seconds.

"I'm sorry for your loss. If you ever need anything, I'm back in town." She sniffed.

"For good?"

She nodded. The door had shut gently as she left. Her Demask rose scent lingered in the air.

Seeing her had been bittersweet. I hadn't shown it, but I'd been pleased to see her. She appeared to be slimmer and weary eyed.

I took a deep sigh of relief. I opened another bottle of Budweiser and went to guzzling it like water. My body was extremely fatigued. My diet consisted of Chinese food, pizza, and Lil Debbie cakes, and I consumed more alcohol than vegetables.

41

I took a seat at my desk hoping I could muster anything onto a word document. I typed some words, hit the backspace key, swallowed some beer. Repeat cycle. Five empty beer bottles later I was still at square one. Not even a single poem or a piece of crappy fiction. I was stumped. "Son of a bitch." I chucked a bottle against the wall. I shielded my face as small shards of glass hailed all over the room. Glass was scattered on the floor and all over my bed. The door swung open with force.

"Don't come in!" I yelled. Jordan peeked inside.

"What's going on?" he asked.

"Nothing. I dropped a bottle. When did you get here?" I asked.

"About three minutes ago."

"Cool. Get the broom and dustpan for me."

I heard my phone vibrating on my bed, so I tiptoed across the floor until I made it to the bed. I shook the blanket to unravel the phone. A fragment of glass pierced through the skin of my palm. "Dammit," I exclaimed as I sucked blood from the cut. Jordan placed the broom near the door. I checked my phone. Benu had sent a text: **Come over babe. I gotta see you.**

I put on a pair of shoes and walked through the living room. I paced through the house searching for my keys. I stepped on the cereal Ashlyn kept flinging on the floor. Jordan found my keys on the TV stand. I was too drunk to travel anywhere, but I had to see my love.

My vision was blurry, but I was aware of my surroundings. The light drizzle was refreshing. I loved the way raindrops tapped the top of my head. I felt fine as I took a stepped onto the road. I looked left, right, left again and proceeded across the street. I slipped on a wet spot, but I caught my fall. Suddenly, I was stunned by the fluorescent headlights of a speeding car coming near. I used my arm to shield my eyes.

"Get yo' dumbass off the road," the driver yelled, pounding the horn, but not slowing. I briefly regained consciousness.

"Holy shit," I shouted. I dove and landed near the curb. The red Mustang sped by like a cheetah. I remained horizontal to the curb; until I saw a flash of red and blue lights. I crawled to the sidewalk and under a nearby tree. I became dizzy by the sirens and flashing lights. The cop vehicles raced down the street so fast all I saw was a blur.

I stood and brushed my clothes off. I rolled the sleeves of my sweater, blood was dripping from my elbow.

I hobbled the block to make my way to the nearest bus stop. I took a seat on the wet bench. I didn't care about anything. I wanted to be next to Benu.

"Yo, Price," someone shouted from his window as he drove by.

There's nothing more embarrassing than getting spotted at the bus stop while it's raining. Nothing pisses me off more than someone not offering a ride when they see me waiting for the bus in the rain.

The light drizzle became a ferocious cold downpour within a blink of an eye. I sat stiffly like a statue, waiting and waiting, and waiting for the bus to come. The bus arrived eight minutes later.

I stepped on the bus dripping water all over the floor. The dark, muscular driver covered the coin slot with her hand as I attempted to put the money in. She must have felt sorry for me. I took a seat in the far back corner.

A few stops later two homeless men boarded the bus. They were bickering over the last portion of their honey bun. I put in my earphones in to tune out the noise. They sat and continued to argue. Even though they were seated far away, their stench hit my nose hard like a ninety-five mile per hour fastball. As I watched the men tug over the snack, one of them caught my eye. He was six feet and two inches with broad shoulders. His face was covered with inches of beard, and his afro was wide and nappy. I turned my music off to see if I could recognize his voice.

"Go to hell, Ray," one bum said to the other.

"Shit, I'd rather go there than to sit here with yo' goofy ass."

My eyes lit up as his voice registered to me. I got a better glimpse of the bum's face, and it was my old man. What a damn day. First, my mother's death, then Iris' engagement and to top this shit flavored cake, my father was a street dweller.

I slouched over until my chest touched my knees. I didn't want him to spot me. My father and the other drifter exited the bus a few stops later. I moved to the front.

I arrived at my stop and got off the bus. I had a few blocks to walk to get to Bee's apartment. The downtown bar strip was crowded for a Wednesday night. I even ran

45

into a few classmates from high school. They tried to converse with me, but I didn't care about what they had to say. I was too damp and cold to hold a cordial conversation. The muscles in my legs were becoming stiff. I was beginning to lose control of my entire body.

A sudden jolt of joy rushed through my spine when I knocked on her door. She was going to make my day worth living. I smiled until my eyes disappeared when the door cracked open.

"Oh my god, you're soaked. Why didn't you ask me to scoop you?"

"I didn't think of it," I shrugged.

"Don't worry, baby. Leave your clothes here and hop in the shower. I'll make some hot tea."

I stripped naked and left my clothes at the door

"Nice ass." She laughed devilishly.

"Stop being a perv."

I took a hot shower and lathered my body with black African soap. Benu eventually invited herself in, too. She lathered my skin with her angel soft hands. We kissed as speckles of warm water ran down her back. We showered together for ten minutes.

She left the shower then wrapped her body and hair in a towel and went to her room.

I stepped out the showered and didn't care about the water dripping onto the floor. I tiptoed to the medicine cabinet. I was anxious to see what those prescription bottles were filled with. I slowly drew the door back, but the bottles were missing.

"Dammit." I snapped my fingers. *Damn, I hope she doesn't have AIDS.*

After I had dried off, I entered her room wearing nothing but a towel. She was watching *House M.D.* on Netflix; another one of my favorite series, because I understood House's pain. She was positioned upwards with her pillow placed to support her back. I rested in her lap. She had the cutest face as she locked in on the television screen. Her eyes would slightly poke out, and her mouth would subtly pucker as if she was about to give me a kiss. Her laugh was so cute, and I adored how she was comfortable enough to pick her nose around me.

I was beginning to love the quirky things about her. I wasn't ready to let my guard down again. The thought of being in love brought anxiety. Love makes people weak, yet somehow strong. It's an empowering yet confusing emotion. Love is a dangerous blessing.

Once the episode ended, she gazed into my eyes and saw the pain on my face. "Bae, what's wrong?" she asked.

"My mom."

"What?"

"She died. She died of an overdose."

"Wow. I'm sorry." She kissed my lips and rubbed my facial hair. I closed my eyes, suddenly two teardrops landed on my forehead.

"I'll be fine," I assured.

"But, I feel so bad."

I rolled over to the right side of the bed. She cuddled under my arm. She was so soft I couldn't help but to squeeze her tight. I held her like I wasn't going to see her again. For once in my life, I had found someone who cared.

"There's one more thing."

"Go on."

"I saw my father on the bus tonight, and he's a homeless bum now," I said.

She chuckled softly, but I didn't mind; because it was hilarious.

"That's crazy. What did you

say?"

"Nothing."

"You had such a crappy day." She kissed my hand.

"Yup, but you've made it worth living."

"Aw, baby. Good night."

"Good night…love you," I whispered.

I got nothing but silence in return.

I'm such a loser, I said to myself.

We cuddled until we fell asleep.

Hours later heavy banging came from the door. Benu jumped and I followed. When she opened the door, Melanie and Cam walked in. They were both loud and unsteady. Cam's face was flushed, and Melanie was squirming in her shorts. Cam walked past Benu to give me a hug. I pushed him away. He playfully jabbed at me. Melanie rushed to the bathroom.

"I'm so happy to see you, bro." He shook me by the shoulders.

"I can tell."

"Hey, I got two tickets to the Yo Gotti show tomorrow."

49

"Good for you." I nodded.

"And I know you love Yo Gotti. So, let's go bro style."

"I don't like his music at all, not even a little bit," I said.

"You're right. He kinda sucks. thinking about selling them."

I shook my head and excused myself from the conversation and went back to Benu's room. She'd crawled back to bed fifteen minutes later. That night I slept next to Benu, but I found myself thinking about Iris. I didn't know why, and I didn't like it. There I was lying next to a queen, but my mind was on the woman who'd hurt me.

GOD HATES ME

The next morning, I awoke to Benu tracing my chest with her finger. *I could wake up to this face every day*, I thought. She was beautiful, even in the morning, without the fake lashes and makeup.

I rolled over to the other side of the bed. Her iPhone poked my back. I recovered it to check the time. It was 10:48. I narrowed my eyes as I gazed at the screenlock photo. It was a picture of man kissing her cheek. She was glowing with joy. My jaw clenched, and my breathing got heavier.

"Hey, who is this?" I asked.

"Who?"

"On your phone."

"Oh, my brother," she answered. "He got killed a few years ago."

My jealousy immediately evaporated. "Sorry to hear," I offered.

"It's fine. The street life caught up to him."

I noticed the fine cuts on her wrist as she snatched her phone away. She also had cigarette burns on her forearms. She caught me grimacing at the scratches and covered her arm.

"Why did you do it?" I asked.

"Do what?" She looked away.

"Don't play dumb. Why'd you try to kill yourself?"

"I love hard and when someone breaks my heart, I tend to fall off the edge," she said.

A million thoughts ran through my brain in a short amount of time. I knew two suicidal lovebirds would make for a perfect story in print, but it was a recipe for disaster in real life.

"Your clothes are in the dryer," she said, and I used the opportunity to leave the room. I dressed in the bathroom and paced for a couple of minutes. I had a hunch something terrible was going to happen, so I created an excuse to leave. I rushed out the bathroom.

"Yo, Bee, I gotta go. My brother got in a school fight," I shouted.

"How would you know?" she asked in an ironic tone.

"Because he-" I patted my pockets and found them empty. I smacked my forehead. I knew I was in for some deep shit. I dashed back into her room. I came to a sudden halt when I saw her peering at my phone with her mouth scrunched up. She drew her eyes to me as I stood there as rigid as a pole and shaking.

"Whose Iris?" she asked.

"Iris?"

"Yeah, Iris. And why does she want to see you?"

"She's an old friend. I haven't spoken to her in years."

"Years? Why did she text: **once again sorry for your loss. It was nice seeing you. Hope to see you soon, as always love you**."

"I should have known to put a lock on my phone," I mumbled.

"Explain Price."

I stumbled over my words as my upper lip quivered. My armpits began to perspire. She made me feel like a cheating boyfriend, but I wasn't.

Her lively eyes turned in pools of rage. "She knew about your mother before me?" She gripped my phone tightly. I shrugged.

"She randomly showed up to my house."

"That whore was at your house?" Her eyes narrowed.

I gave a shaky smile. "Bee, it's not like that." I waved my hands.

She cocked her arm back as if he was readying to throw a tight spiral. My phone came towards me faster than a silver bullet. I swiftly ducked to my right. The cellular device smashed against the art piece she had hanging on the wall. The impact imposed a small dent on the painting. Folds began to form on her forehead.

I retrieved my phone. "I have to go now," I said. I walked sideways with my back against the wall as I made my way out. I gently closed the door behind me.

I ran a few blocks away from her apartment complex to make sure she wasn't trailing me. I pulled my phone out of my pocket. The screen was shattered, but I could see it well enough to request an Uber ride. My sweater was inside out, but I didn't care. My mouth was dry, and my lungs were out of oxygen. I had realized how out of shape I was. I noticed the driver, Donell, staring at me through his mirror.

"What, man?" I asked.

He placed his attention back on the road.

"Nothing. You look tired," he said with a heavy southern accent.

"Tired of life."

"You better relax and be grateful." He tossed a bottle of water to the back seat. I twisted the cap off and guzzled it to the halfway mark. I took a deep breath of satisfaction. I took off my shirt to switch it right side out. He lowered the radio volume.

"What's gotten you so beat?" he asked.

"My girl, well she's more of a friend, but I found out she's bat shit crazy."

"Leave her ass, man. Leave her while you can."

"But..."

"But nothing," he snapped. "The problem with you young folks; y'all think being overly jealous and possessive is cute."

"Yo, you ran a red light." I grabbed his shoulder.

"Let me finish." He shrugged me off and continued. "Y'all think it's cute for your girl to be crazy until the day you're in jail." "What?"

"Yeah. A crazy woman does nothing but bring the crazy out of you. She could hit you five hunnit thousand times, but if you break so much as a fingernail of hers yo' ass goin' to jail. Trust me, I've been there."

"You've been to jail?"

He nodded vigorously. "Five times. All over a crazy bitch."

"I thought Uber drivers were supposed to have clean records," I said.

"Mann, you are worried about the wrong thing right now. Back to what I said, leave her ass."

After running three red lights and one stop sign, we arrived at the destination. I told him to come back in two hours and gave a five-star rating despite the fact he'd put my life in danger.

There were four loitering bums outside of the venue. They all begged for money, but I declined. I didn't want to support their alcohol habit; I wanted to support mine.

I walked through the broken door of 'Somethin Different' locally dubbed as 'The Dirty.' It was a hole-in-the-wall bar, dimly lit with a humid atmosphere. It was a place you could enter, but leaving wasn't guaranteed. It was a place where hardcore addicts could drink, snort, and shoot without being judged. I only went there because they played good music, and was located a few blocks away from my home.

I took a seat and requested the usual, gin on the rocks. An elderly woman sat next to me. She reeked of two-day-old garbage and Black & Mild's.

"Hey, handsome. Looking for some fun?" She whispered in my ear. I flinched at the sound of her raspy voice.

"I'm sure I wouldn't find it with you." I leaned away from her. She inched closer.

"I'm running a thirty-dollar special," she said.

"Thirty dollars? You're selling pussy for thirty dollars?" I asked as I wiped the spittle off my chin. She nodded with a raised eyebrow. "You'd be better off working as a telemarketer."

She huffed, stormed away from the bar. She broke a heel as she stomped across the floor. For an hour, she tried to solicit fellow bar patrons. I felt bad for her. She had to feel worthless, because she failed to sell pussy.

After a relentless effort, she finally found a buyer. The guy stood six feet and six inches tall, dark, and well-built; so, I was a little shocked to see a good-looking guy stoop so low. My stomach boiled a little bit as they held hands and walked to the bathroom.

"So, you guys let her do business here?" I asked the bartender. She shrugged then refilled my glass. "Fine establishment you guys have here."

About thirty minutes later Donell came inside to pick me up. I purchased a whiskey on the rocks for him then we stepped out. He sipped on the drink as he turned the ignition. I wanted to say something, but I kept my mouth shut.

We arrived at my house a few minutes later. Jordan was mowing the lawn. A pleasant surprise because yard work was a foreign chore to him. His dark hair was tied in a ponytail. He was panting like a dehydrated dog. I went inside to pour a glass of water for him. Ashlyn was on the couch kicking in her sleep. Jordan came inside. He placed his hand on his knees as he gasped for air. I handed him the cup. He gulped the water without taking a breath.

"I cleaned the house and mowed the lawn to make sure this place is in decent shape when mom gets back," he said. He used his palm to wipe the dripping water from the sides of his mouth. I embraced him. He looked from the side of his eyes. "What? You never hug me. Is everything okay?" he asked. I chuckled.

"Everything's good." I tapped his chest softly. "I'm going to my room. Let me know if you need anything," I said.

As I walked to my room, I noticed the birthday decorations dangling from the door seals. There were balloons tied to the table legs.

"Is today Ash's birthday?" I asked Jordan.

"Next week, but mom's birthday is tomorrow."

"Oh."

Every day was so much of a blur they all felt the same. I had no reason to keep up with dates or events. I placed my hands on my hips and shook my head. I went to my room and sat on the edge of my mattress. It had finally hit me. My mother was gone, and she was never coming back. I placed my hands to my face.

Tears began to seep through the cracks of my fingers as I cried uncontrollably. She was my beautiful mother. Far from perfect, but she meant well. She had been perfect before she'd met Thomas. He was a tornado that stormed and terrorized us for fifteen years, leaving the foundation of my family in shambles.

I felt sorry for my siblings. They'd never been given the opportunity to meet the mother who would take them to the park, kiss them good night, and cook Sunday dinner for them, but I had. I'd almost taken those memories for granted.

I was stuck taking care of two children while battling my own ordeals, I knew how she'd felt. I was a budding alcoholic who dove inside any pussy that gave me a warm welcome. I was alone and a few weeks away from killing myself. Life was spiraling out of my hands.

First, my girlfriend, Gianna, had dumped me, and my third novel had flopped. Next, I'd lost my job and the few friends I had, my mother died, Iris was engaged, Benu was a psycho, and my only source of income was writing essays for college students.

Gianna was this West Indian goddess who donned long jet-black hair that flowed over her shoulders. Her face was perfectly slanted. Her five-seven frame was complimented with succulent curves. Her thick Guyanese accent was more beautiful than any song I had ever heard. What I loved the most about her was the scar, a symbol of her imperfection, on the right of her forehead.

We'd met at a house party through mutual friends shortly after I'd cut ties with Iris. At first, we hadn't hit it off. I was socially awkward, and she was too high maintenance.

One day she called and asked, "Do you write poetry?" I said, "yes." She recited a few of her poems, I recited a few of mine. I remember the first poem I read to her.

I am nothing without love

Which means I am nothing without you

Come find me

Wherever you are

I need to feel wanted

I want to feel important

I need your motivation

Because you're everything I need

And I am nothing without you

It had been a decent piece, nothing spectacular, but she'd loved it. At first, we started off as friends. She admired me, but only platonically. The more time we spent together, the deeper my feelings grew. She was barely eighteen, but full of wisdom. I was eternally indebted to her for being my light in a world of darkness. She helped me find the piece of me that had gone dormant after Iris. She eventually fell for my charm and we became two best friends who were in love.

We were together for eighteen months. I remember when we first made love. Her long legs were wrapped around my waist as I stroked inside of her. Her pussy reminded me of heaven, and I never wanted to leave.

My mission was to make her happier than she was the previous day, until one day we got into our first major dispute. When I told her, I was quitting my decent paying job to pursue my dream, she'd uttered, "I refuse to struggle with you." Those words resonated with me for many days and nights. When the love of your life doesn't support your passion, a piece of you dies. She hollowed me from the inside out and I became a shell of myself.

I was her first, and she'd said we were going to die together. Instead, forever hadn't lasted long, and I was the one who'd died when she'd left. The way she'd left had made me feel as if I held no value to her life. She had tossed my love away like an old newspaper. She was gone swifter than a daydream, and our memories were nothing but a past time.

My life was becoming a downwards spiral of mayhem, and I had nowhere to turn.

Jordan entered my room and sat next to me. His eyes wandered the room. "So, she's not coming?" he asked. "Is she ever coming back home?"

I looked at my little brother, but a single word didn't come out. He saw my misty eyes and knew the answer.

"She's gone, Jay," I finally said. He curled his bottom lip and begun softly tugging on his long hair.

"Where is she?" he asked.

I withdrew the silver urn from under my bed and handed it to him. He cradled the urn with his hands and stared in dismay. He didn't flinch or blink.

"That's crazy."

"Life is crazy." I stretched across my bed. "Don't tell Ash yet, okay?" I said.

"To be honest, she wouldn't even notice the difference," he said. He stood. "I love you, bro."

"I love you more," I said.

He left my room. I was shaken. I checked my banking account and became even more depressed when I glared at the overdraft of seventy-seven dollars.

I laid to rest my weary eyes. My thoughts were swimming through my mind a mile a minute. I thought about my mother, and how her soul could finally be free from the poison that killed her. I thought of my street-dwelling father and wondered if I would ever see him again, because I needed him now more than ever. And the women of my dysfunctional love life came across my brain. The women who seemed so perfect were the ones who usually hurt you the most, but I wasn't looking for perfect, I was looking for someone genuine.

I rolled over and planted my face into my pillow until I was suffocated by the scent of hot breath and alcohol. Gentle taps sounded on the door, but I tried to ignore them.

"Price," Iris said through the door crack. Her heels clanked against the concrete floor as she approached my bed. "C'mon, I'm not stupid," she said as she laughed at my phony snoring.

"What do you want?" I muttered through the pillow. Her breasts were pressing against my back. I tried to wiggle her off, but she managed to straddle me. "I can feel your pussy on my back," I said. She wore a floral print romper, and her hair flowed over her shoulders.

"I hate you," She slapped my back, and laid on the other side of the bed. We briefly looked at each other. My head was turned to her as she lay on her back.

"These sheets smell like nights of shame. When's the last time you changed them?" she asked.

I took a whiff. "You're right. I haven't changed them since four women ago."

"You're such a slut."

"I'm only living my life. There should be some sheets in there." I gestured at the top drawer of the high dresser. She quickly went to retrieve the bed spreads. I stood to the side as she stripped my mattress and swapped the smelly sheets with the clean ones. She began picking up clothes, trash, and empty beer bottles.

"Ew. You bring women here?"

"Not during the day."

She laughed. She gathered all the cleaning materials we had and went to work. She got on her hands and knees and scrubbed every cranny of the room. I couldn't help but stare at her as she would often arch her back as she mopped the floor. That romper accentuated her lovely shape. She found my lost 808's and Heartbreak album when she swept debris and old junk from under my bed.

"If I could I would pay for your lunch right now," I said.
"You don't have any money?" she pouted.

"I have negative seventy-seven dollars."

"I'll give you the money and we'll have lunch on me."

"Thanks. What brought you here anyways?" I asked.

"I wanted to see you." She cleared her throat. "To see how you're holding up, I mean."

"I'm good. You ready?" I asked. She nodded.

"Okay. I'll meet you outside."

I put on a change of clothes and even switched my two-day old boxers. Jordan and Ashlyn were on the couch playing connect four. I was starting to feel horrible. I was spending more time at the bar or with women than with my own siblings when they needed me more than ever. I was too busy being consumed by my own misery. I was a big baby who was at the legal drinking age. Leaving Jordan to take care of Ashlyn wasn't fair. He deserved to have some sort of normalcy. Instead, he was stuck taking care of his disabled sister while worrying about his alcoholic brother. I hugged them and rushed out the door.

"Hey, your fly is open," Iris said as I entered the car.

"Gotta let it breathe down there,"
I responded.

"You're so silly." She rolled her neck.

"I like what you've done with your hair, by the way."

"Oh, you noticed?"

"Always." I winked.

Her smile quickly disappeared as she turned her attention to the road. I raised the radio volume to avoid the awkward silence. We sang along with the songs for the rest of the ride.

Iris and I went downtown for some ice cream. We walked along the pier nearby the waterfront. Typically, drops of sweat would be dripping from my forehead, but not that day. The weather was soothing. Gust of soft winds blew against the trees. Sea foam waves splashed on the rocks. The sky was clear, and the sun blazed blistering hot. She asked about my books, and I told her my sales were miserable. She said I was a phenomenal writer, one of her favorites. It meant a lot coming from her since the women of my stories bared her essence.

I reached for her hand. Her fingertips gently touched against mine. I quickly withdrew my hand before our palms locked.

67

We proceeded to stroll downtown. We laughed and reminisced about the memories we'd shared. Thunder began to roar, followed by a ferocious downpour of cold raindrops. We immediately ran for the nearest cover. We found a closed store with an overhead to shield ourselves. She was shivering, so I gave her my sweater and wrapped my arm around her.

"Florida weather, right?" I said.

"Never know what you're gonna get next," she retorted.

We waited until the rain settled into a light drizzle.

"Wait here so I can get the car," I

said,

"Can you even drive?"

"Duh. Of course, I can drive. Give me the keys," I said.

She placed the keys inside my palm and I scurried away. A rush of nervousness jolted through my body when I sat in the driver's seat. My forearms shook as I gripped the steering wheel. I hit the gas pedal, but the vehicle refused to move.

"C'mon. What the hell?" I said. I stomped on the pedal, but the key wasn't in the ignition.

I'd never been much of a driver. My anxiety always went into overdrive whenever I got behind the wheel. My fear of dying behind the wheel consumed me so much to the point I avoided hitting the road. Unlike most kids, my parents had not been around to teach me how to drive. Even when I had friends, I didn't give them the chance to teach me because I had been too ashamed to ask.

"I knew you couldn't drive." Iris smiled as she got in on the passenger's side. "You would always make excuses not to drive my car back in the day."

"I can drive," I said as I cranked the engine.

"No, you can't and it's okay. You never had anyone around long enough to teach you. I got you," she said. "Now, relax and put the car in reverse. Keep your foot on the breaks," she instructed.

"I know the basic steps, alright," I said.

"Well, if you knew so much you wouldn't be here shivering in your drawls right now."

"I'm cold from the rain."

"Right." She laughed. "Price, I'll teach you how to drive." She told me to shut up and listen. Iris guided me during the whole ride. My heart went racing fifty miles per second, but she made me feel more comfortable. She'd always possessed such a calming presence as well. She could make me feel secure amidst a firestorm. I'd never understood why I had such immense feelings for her, and I despised it. She possessed the ability to bring the best out of me. It was her gift.

After a short and jarring ride, we arrived at her condominium complex which oversaw the skyline of downtown. Her unit was on the highest floor.

"Living large for an educational worker," I said.

"My fiancé paid for this, jackass," she said as she unlocked the door.

"Sorry. I almost forgot about him," I responded.

She scowled as we entered her condo. I took a seat on their red velvet couch. I glanced at the décor and noticed the quotes hanging on the walls and replicas of Greek statues posted in each corner. *Only a pretentious douche would live here*, I thought.

Iris called for her fiancé, Ramone, but she received no response. She called his name again.

"What, babe? I'm on the shitter." His voice echoed from down the hall.

"Okay," she called back. "I'll get you some scotch," she told me.

"I need it bad," I responded as she walked to the kitchen.

"Well, well, well, if it's not the next great American novelist himself," Ramone said, as he walked into the living room. He was brawny and made sure to showcase his muscles by wearing a tank top so tight it probably constricted his blood flow. The ceiling lights reflected off his freshly shaved head. He stood 6'6; his chest was doused with baby powder which made me chuckle on the inside.

He had a copy of my latest book clutched to his hip. "You're one bad son of a bitch. Whenever I take I dump, I bring one of your books with me," he said with his thick Latin accent.

"Thanks, but hey I didn't hear any water running from the sink, though," I replied.

"What are you getting at, eh?" "Forget about it," I answered.

"Babe, would you like a drink?" Iris asked.

"I thought you were already making me one," I responded. "I'm joking,"

I said to Ramone and reached for a handshake. His hand was strong enough to crack my bones.

Iris placed the drinks on the coasters in front of us. She wore a frown of disappointment as she slowly walked away.

"What's with the long face, mi Amor?" he asked.

"Nothing," she replied.

"Compliment her hair," I whispered. Iris had her back facing us, but I saw a smile from the side of her face.

"I love what you've done to the hair," Ramone said.

"Thank you, Rammy." She smiled. "I'm so glad you guys are getting along. It means a lot to me," she continued as she walked to the kitchen.

"Yeah, of course," I said as I sucked on the liquor. "Look, I have to go. It was nice meeting you Ramone.

"Likewise, my friend. Hope to see you again soon."

"And thanks for everything today, Iris."

"Is everything okay?" she asked. "No, it's not," I answered.

I left without saying goodbye, and didn't bother to look back. Meeting Ramone was the equivalent of getting shitted on by a pigeon. I was an idiot for allowing myself to catch feelings. I had a soft spot for her and she knew it. *She's about to marry some Rico Sauvé who doesn't even notice when she gets her hair done,* I thought aloud.

I took a bus ride home, so I could have a moment to clear my thoughts. I thought, *what did I do to deserve such bullshit?* The feeling of being unwanted is a miserable one. It makes you feel worthless. It makes you wonder if you're the bad guy. And that's how I felt. I'd convinced myself this earth and everyone around me was better off, without me.

When I arrived home, there was a lime green Porsche parked in the driveway. Which was strange to see. I trotted to the door and unlocked it. There was a man hugging Jordan as I walked in, and another sitting next to Ashlyn on the couch. Everyone's attention was directed to me. I saw the guy's face and instantly froze. I lit a cigarette and took a few puffs.

"What a day," I said. "What a damn day."

73

GOD IS A WOMAN

WELL, ISN'T THIS AWKWARD

"Wow haven't you grown into a fine young man," Thomas said as he stepped towards me. I stood stiff and breathless as I stared at his smug expression.

His unpleasant face brought back the heinous memories of him fondling me when I was a kid and how he would punch me in the chest when tears fell from my eyes. He put me in this dark, cold place, and left me there alone with this monster I tried to suppress my entire life. No matter how hard I tried to overcome it, the pain never subsided. And that's how pain operates, it festers until it kills you inside.

"What the fuck are you doing here?" I yelled.

I narrowed my eyes as he began to speak. He said he was in town to reunite with some old friends and introduce his husband to his children. Frankie was a slender dark man and ten years Thomas' junior. Jordan was all smiles; I couldn't understand how a child could be excited to see the father who bailed on him.

I went to the fridge for a beer as Thomas blabbered about his happy life, his loving husband and high successful career as a car salesman. Hearing about his joyful life made me want to punch his teeth out even more. I took large swigs from the beer as his voice bothered my ears. Frankie introduced himself; he seemed a kind fellow. I took a seat next to Jordan and Ashlyn on the couch. I remained quiet and sipped my beer.

I wanted to choke. The audacity to come back in our home and poise and act as if everything is all smiles and giggles was unbearable. I didn't want to make a scene in front of the kids, so I went to my room. I flopped on my bed. The hinges on my door creaked as Jordan entered. His face appeared to be worried as if he had something troubling to say.

"Look, Price, when my dad leaves tonight, we're going with him."

"No. Y'all can't do this to me." I sprang to my feet.

"Bro, you've been taking care of us since you were fifteen years old, now it's time to take care of yourself."

"Y'all all I got."

75

"And we need you to get your life together."

He was right. I was a mess who couldn't take care of himself. My siblings deserved to live in a household where their needs were tended to. Ashlyn needed undivided supervision, but I was too plastered to pay attention half of the time. Jordan needed to focus on his studies, but he was always busy parenting Ashlyn.

I was a burden to myself. My siblings needed guidance, but I was too lost to lead them.

We went back into the living room. Thomas came to me and placed his cold palm on my shoulder. I looked at him with disgust.

"I never told you this, but I'm sorry for everything. I really am." I saw the agony in his eyes. I nodded. The burden of what he had done to me and my mother was slowly chewing him from the inside like acid and he needed to make amends. For once he'd apologized and it was sincere.

Thomas embraced me. Followed by Jordan and Frank. I walked over to Ashlyn and planted a kiss on her cheek. I wasn't sure if I had forgiven him, but I knew I felt better. I excused myself from their presence and went back to my room.

I paced my room with tears streaming down my cheeks. I knew I was going to miss them. They were the only two people keeping me alive. Without them, I had nothing to live for.

Jordan and Ashlyn walked in. I kissed my siblings' goodbye and watched as they pranced. They appeared to be enthused about starting a new life, and I didn't blame them. They deserved to be happy, and I didn't have an ounce of happiness to give.

I stood to my feet as Thomas approached me. "Words can't explain how sorry I am about the damaged I've caused you, but I'll do everything in my power to make it right." Thomas hugged me.

"I'm damaged beyond repair," I responded, as I released him from my clasp. He gave me his contact info and told me if I ever needed anything to not hesitate to call. I knew he couldn't provide anything I needed. I needed an inner healing, and God couldn't fix my demons.

When I looked up, Thomas was gone. A tight knot hit my stomach, once I heard his Porsche engine rev up. Two hours had slipped away before I realized how late it was. The liquor store was closing soon, so I trotted for eight blocks. I purchased a bottle of Honey

Jack Daniels, and made a quick stop at the gas station for chips and candy. I also purchased the lone newspaper at the stand for the comics and crossword puzzles. I never kept up with the news, because it was nothing, but depression and lies; the last two things I wanted to see or hear.

As I approached the register I heard a voice calling my name. I looked over my shoulder, and there was Gianna standing behind me with her stomach so wide it looked like it was ready to explode any minute. I stood there in silence. Her belly bumped into me as she went for a hug. I gave the cashier my money.

"Wait, you're pregnant?" I stepped to the side.

"What does it look like?" She laughed.

"But we last fucked seven months ago."

"The baby isn't yours." She placed her items on the counter.

Time seemed to freeze. It was like I was in a poorly scripted movie with a prolonged ending. She was all smiles as if she was happy to see me. She swiped her debit card. I stared at her as I tried to process everything in my head. I was not her first and our whole relationship had been based on a lie.

"Where's the lucky guy?" I asked.

"In jail."

"Oh, how classic."

"Well, it was nice seeing you. I wish you the best."

She waddled out the door like my feelings meant nothing. I saw no remorse in her eyes. She hadn't even apologized. An admission of guilt would've been like putting a band-aid on a gunshot wound anyways. Apologies do nothing, but remind the receiver how gullible they were for falling for someone's bullshit.

"I feel your pain," the clerk said.

"Yup, God is on fire today," I responded.

I'd already chugged one-fourth of the bottle before I got home. My back and knees were in excruciating pain. I went to my mother's old room to raid her medicine cabinet. I popped four Vicodin and washed them down with a swig of Jack Daniels. I went back to my room and read the comics and solved a few word puzzles. As I flipped the sections, the headline *Homeless Man Found Dead in Dumpster* grabbed my attention. I continued to read:

Local homeless man, Gary Simon Jones, 50, was found dead in a dumpster on 34th Avenue and 6th Street. He suffered seventeen stab wounds. There are no leads to the murder.

My father's corpse had been discovered three blocks away from my home, and no one knew anything. I swallowed three more pills and took another swig from my bottle then I began to type.

To whoever reads this over my deteriorated body,

As I sit here in this cold dusky room nothing is clear to me. I don't think anything has been clear since I was ten-years-old. I'm more comfortable amid the darkness than I am around people. People do nothing but inflict damage like a hurricane and think sayin, "I'm sorry" will fix everything. Well, it doesn't. Once the rain subsides, and the wind drifts away we're left with the shattered debris to remind us of what transpired. I've come to the harsh realization I no longer matter to anyone. I'm like my father. What kind of life is that? Everything I touch turns to shit. I've tried to repress my anger. I've tried to remain positive, but God continues to take a massive crap on me. I often question if God is real because if there was such a being why she would allow anyone to live with this kind of pain? Yes, God is a woman and she's making me feel her wrath. I'm feeling weary and I'm losing my touch. The sky is falling, and it is time to go to bed now. Hopefully for good,

Love, Price

I put "Heart-shaped Box" by Nirvana on repeat and allowed the song bleed through the stereo. I laid back and closed my eyes and inhaled deeply. Hoping I took my last breath.

THE LESS I FEEL, THE BETTER

I woke up in a bright cold room lying on top of a hard brick mattress. My balls hung freely in a hospital gown. Fluids from an IV flowed through my veins.

"Thank God you're awake." I heard Iris' voice from the corner of the room. I turned my head slowly and glanced at her. She looked tired and worn out. Her hair was frizzy, and her make-up was smudged all over the pillow next to her. I was flustered.

"What happened?" I croaked out.

"You almost killed yourself."

"Another thing I failed at." I chuckled dryly.

"Why were you trying to die, Price?"
"Because I have nothing to live for."

"Stop talking, please," she said, making her way towards the bed. "You have me, and the beautiful gift you are so hell-bent on pissing away,"

"I don't have you and I never will."
"I told you I will always be here for you."
"You can leave now."
"No," she said firmly. "I'm going to get you better then I'll let you go."
"Deal."
"You promise you'll let me?" she insisted.
"Yeah, I promise."
"Let's shake on it," she said. We shook hands.

A few hours later, we checked out. I had no medical insurance, so Iris insisted on covering the bill. She took me to breakfast and even paid the bill.

I had been hospitalized for five days after nearly fading to my death. Iris had been there praying for me each night. I owed her everything. While we ate, she told me her fiancé left for a business trip and I could crash with her for a few weeks.

The season had changed to fall, and the month was October, and I could feel the autumn breeze coming in. I always loved the fall season. The weather always created a state of solace.

Iris gushed when I told her how gorgeous she was. She tried to downplay the compliment because that's how she was; a humbled spirit who took nothing for granted. Her bottom lips curled. She had a lingering smile. She tried to erase it, but the compliment flattered her.

She took me to my place, so I could gather enough clothes, then took me to her place. She had an extra room with a bed for me to lay in. I unpacked my belongings and charged my phone. Once my battery had enough juice the notifications began buzzing. I saw the fifty-eight unread text messages and fifteen voicemails from Benu. I tried to call her, but her phone was disconnected.

I went to visit her and told her about my failed suicide attempt. She didn't look well. Her skin was pale, and she appeared frail and tired. She was sleep deprived and hadn't eaten much the whole time I'd been gone. She told me she was sick and would seek help soon, she was stronger than me, because I was too afraid to admit I had a problem. She let me read the labels on her medicine bottles. She had been prescribed Anxiolytic, Escitalopram, and

Risperidone. She was going back home to be with her family and check into a mental health institution.

I spent a few hours with her; we laughed, we danced, and painted together.

When I left her apartment, I knew an era had ended. Life is like that sometimes. People will come in your life and bring you instant joy like a rainbow or wreak havoc like a hurricane. And once their duty is done their presence will fade away leaving you to live alone.

Benu had been my rainbow and my hurricane. I never saw her again.

I made it back to Iris' place and she left for work shortly after. I raided her cabinets for the booze, but I couldn't find any. I left her place to go to the liquor store. My phone buzzed so I checked the message. It was from Iris.

If you haven't noticed yet, I took your debit card and ID, so you won't make any quick trips to the liquor store ☺. And one more thing I left $10 on the counter, in case you get hungry later.

Son of a monkey, I said to myself.

I went back to the condo and watched television since there was nothing left to do. I even tried to write something. As per usual, nothing came out of me. I grew bored and began snooping around. I discovered a yellow folder concealed underneath a pile of school books in the guest closet. Out of curiosity, I opened the folder. I flipped through the first few sheets of paper until I realized; they were the letters and poems I'd dedicated to Iris during our fling. After so long she'd kept my undying infatuation in her possession. Each poem was laminated. I smiled at the delicacy in which she'd handled my work. I put everything back in order and went to watch cartoons until she got home.

Iris arrived home after six o'clock. She dressed down to yoga pants and a tee shirt.

"Get dressed, you lazy bum," she said. "You're coming with me."

"Where?"

"Yoga class," she said.

"Not my thing." I shook my head.

"It's gonna be your thing every Tuesday and Thursday. Get used to it."

I got dressed and we jogged the trail until we arrived at the yoga studio. I dropped to my hands and knees gasping for air. My hamstrings were on fire.

"We only jogged a quarter of a mile, Price. Stop being dramatic." She laughed.

"I am about to – "I spewed vomit on the concrete. "-die." I said, wiping vomit from my mouth.

"You'll be fine." She gave me a few minutes to collect myself. We went inside the studio, and she purchased three bottles of water. I grabbed two yoga mats.

The instructor, Janie, stood five six with a lean physique and a plump ass. She wore her hair in a bun. As she began the lesson, I couldn't keep my eyes off her ass as she stretched in various positions.

Iris gave me a side-eyed scowl as I ogled Janie. She showed a faint hint of jealousy and it was cute. It made me feel good.

My muscles were far from limber as I struggled to perform each pose. I was uncoordinated and stiff. Women gave me side eyed glances when I tumbled to the floor every forty-five seconds. I was the only male, and I was embarrassed. My build was lean, but I had the flexibility of an elephant and the endurance of a cheap battery.

After the yoga session, Iris and I took the trail back to her condo. This time we power walked. The weather was breezy. Nothing felt better than an autumn evening.

"Yo Iris, I meant to ask you. Why were you at my house?"

"What do you mean?"

"The day you found my body, you were at my house. Why?"

"Me and Ramone got into a huge

fight." "About what?"

"It's not important. What is important is how I found you in time to save your life."

"I didn't want to be saved."

"I had to. Seeing you foaming at the mouth with your body shuddering brought me to tears. I couldn't lose you."

"Like you care."

"Price, I do care. You may find it impossible to believe, but I still care about you."

I took a breather on a nearby bench. She sat next to me.

"I read your suicide note," she said. "Oh,

that thing." I shrugged.

"Price, you're a beautiful man and a genuine human. You deserve to know."

"Thanks, but I'm beyond fixing. I'm nothing but damaged goods."

"I wish I had the world's smallest violin to play right now," she said.

I laughed. "I hate you so much," I said. She smiled back and gave me a playful nudge.

We stood, and power walked the rest of the way to her place. A slight gust of wind gave her the chills so, I wrapped my arm around her. We played the constellation game as we gazed at the star-filled sky. Years ago,

we would lay on top of her car while tracing shapes in the sky. I missed those moments.

Once we arrived at her place, we showered, not together, of course. She prepared: a tropical parfait, garden salad, and lentil soup for dinner. It was far from Shrimp Lo Mein and Hawaiian pizza, but it did the stomach well.

She graded papers as I watched a low budget film entitled *Mama's Foot*. The film was god-awful. I had no clue as to why I tortured myself by watching it. I took a sip of her warm tea. It hit my chest so well.

"Hey, Price, so you like kids?" she asked.

"Hell, yeah. I love the little snotty-nosed bastard. They're wonderful."

"Great, because I can get you a job as a tutor."

"I could use the money."

"Cool. Have your resume ready in the morning. You'll be working in no time."

"Aren't you supposed to have some stupid degree to be a teacher or a tutor?"

"You're a novelist. It's better than having a degree."

She finished grading her assignments and went to her bedroom. I remained in the living room. I stretched, did pushups and sit ups and tried to write. I pumped out a few subpar poems; which felt a rhino had been lifted off my back.

I rushed to Iris's room and called her name as I entered. Iris was in her bed with a towel around her waist, I covered an eye. She was Facetiming her fiancé.

"Who the hell?" Ramone asked.

"My brother," she answered. I gave a thumb up.

"Oh, tell my boy, Allen, I said I miss him," he said.

"I miss you too, man," I responded. Iris threw me a scolding look.

"I love him so man," Ramone laughed to her. He asked for the camera to be switched to me. I quickly walked back to my room. Ten minutes later Iris came to my room wrapped in a cashmere robe.

"What did you want, asshole?" she

asked. "Where's my ID? I want to

celebrate." "Celebrate what?"

"My writer's block is over, well kinda. I wrote something. It was crap, but I wrote something."

"Good but I'm not giving your ID back."

"Why not?"

"Because you're in rehab now."

"You suck," I said. She chuckled.

"You'll be fine, Pricey." She pinched my cheek and went back into her bedroom.

I grew unamused and left the condo. I strolled downtown to see if I could find a woman who was the right kind of drunk. I hated when women drank themselves into a stupor. They're so unappealing when they dragged their bare feet across the concrete and used bypassing strangers to keep them upright.

A dark Hispanic woman with deep brown hair flowing over her breasts caught my eye as she exited The Crowbar. I reached for her arm, but she pulled away.

"Excuse me," I said.

"Leave me alone. I have mace." She looked back at me and her eyes widened. "Oh, hey handsome."

"Thank you, I'm Price."

"Mariana." We shook hands.

"May I walk with you?"

"Sure. I'm going to my car." She spoke with a soft lisp on top of her Dominican accent. It was quirky yet attractive.

I was surprised she was comfortable with the idea of a stranger following her. Women have it so hard. They can become a victim of rape or sexual assault because some jerk got his rocks off by attacking vulnerable women.

As we walked, she told me about herself. She was twenty-two, majoring in public health at the University of Florida. She was visiting her family for the weekend, and recovering from a horrible breakup, which meant she was buzzed and heartbroken. A perfect combination. When we reached her car, we sat and talked. The radio was faintly playing.

"You kinda look like him," she said as "Pretty Wings" played.

"Who, Maxwell?"

"Yes. I love him." She bit the tip of her tongue.

"I'll take that as a compliment."

I placed my hand between her thighs. She stared at me when her flirtatious eyes and grabbed my wrist. She guided my hand to her pussy. Her eyes rolled as I massaged her clit. Her moan was so erotic. I reclined in the seat. She straddled me. I lifted her dress and discovered her pussy was uncovered. Mariana unbuckled my belt and undid my zipper.

"Are you sure you wanna do this?" I asked.

"Yes," she gasped. "I need it." She placed my shaft inside her pussy. She began to ride hard and fast as I sucked on her nipple piercings. She ripped my button-up shirt open. I gripped her ass. Her sharp nails clawed my skin, leaving long red marks on my chest. We both came in three and a half minutes.

Mariana went back to the driver's seat. I had her drop me off a block away from Iris's complex.

"It was nice meeting you," I said.

"It was nice fucking you," she responded.

"Bye." I exited the car.

It was approaching one o'clock and Iris was still awake sitting on the couch eating ice cream. She had her hair in a curly bun and wore an oversized t-shirt. I couldn't help but gaze at her simplistic beauty.

"Why are you up?" I asked.

"You weren't responding to my texts, so I wanted to make sure you came back alive."

"Well, there's no way I could've come back dead."

She shook her head. I sat next to her.

"Your zipper is down," she said.

"Why are you always looking at my penis?" I asked.

She rolled her eyes. "And you smell like pussy, again.'"

"Thanks for noticing," I responded.

She reminded me to have my resume ready in the morning and got up to make her way back to her bedroom.

"Goodnight and... happy birthday," I said.

Her smile went cheek to cheek. She was surprised I had remembered, but how could I ever forget?

"Good night," she said and continued walking to her room.

I took another shower to wash the stench off me. I wanted to join Iris bed. I knew she would've welcomed me, but I went to my room instead. I wrote a few more poems then went to bed.

I was at peace knowing someone cared about my well-being. For a long time, I'd lived a life surrounded by people taking from me and taking me for granted. People drained me until I had nothing left. Iris was here to reform me, and I didn't know why. She had her own life and a fiancé. Yet, she'd still come back for me. Her return to my life had a much deeper purpose than what was read on the surface. And she knew it.

GOD IS A WOMAN

HAPPY BIRTHDAY, IRIS

When I awoke the next morning, Iris had already left for work. I ate cereal and watched Stephan A. Smith and Skip Bayless bark at each other for two hours on ESPN's *First Take*. I worked out in the facility's gym for an hour and walked the trail for a mile.

I returned to Iris's condo for a shower and nap. Iris arrived home after five with two sandwiches from PDQ and gave me one. She seemed gloomy and distant. She refused to look at me and barely spoke.

"What's wrong," I asked?

"Nothing." She sighed. "Just a long day."

"Alright." I finished the sandwich and went to the bathroom for a shower. The walls trembled as Iris blasted "Chinatown" by Migos through the sound system. I finished showering and she turned the music down to answer the door.

"Sister," she greeted.

'Sister," the other women greeted.

I'd forgotten she had a sister, and hoped she'd grown to be attractive. I dried my body and put my pants on. I was feeling beefy, so I went to the living room shirtless.

"Hey Iris, could you…. Whoa," I said as I saw the woman."

"She's beautiful, isn't she?" Iris said. "Price, Mariana. Mariana, Price." She introduced us.

"Yeah, she's definitely beautiful." I shook her hand.

"Nice to meet you, Price," She said.

"Likewise." I smiled awkwardly.

"This is Ramone's sister, but I love her like my own." Iris hugged her. "You two would look cute together," Iris suggested. A big silence grew amongst us.

"Well, I gotta go finish some stuff." I rushed off to my room.

I put my ear to the door to eavesdrop on their conversation. Iris told her about our past relationship. She hinted Mariana and I should date, but Mariana was reluctant. I crossed my fingers hoping she would keep her mouth shut about our one-night stand. Iris didn't need to know. As they continued to converse, Iris seemed to be upset about something. I heard it in her tone, but she refused to speak on it as Mariana tried to milk it out of her.

I stopped listening in and got dressed. I was in a cheerful mood as I listened to Stevie Wonder. My spirits could not have been higher. I put on my best attire: a black sweater, black pants, and black vans.

The ladies complimented me as I strutted through the living room. Mariana stared as if she wanted another piece of me.

"Can I get my ID back?" I asked Iris.

"Of course.... not."

"C'mon. Being sober sucks."

"You're our designated driver tonight." She handed me the keys. I snatched them out of her hand and stomped to the door. I was somewhat livid. The last thing I wanted was to be sober amongst a clique of intoxicated women.

We met Iris's friends, Yaya' and Naomi, at The Crowbar. Yaya' was short, dark, with straight medium hair. I knew her from my past. Her sex had been decent, but her head had been life-changing. I still get hot flashes when I think about her lips sliding up and down my shaft. And Naomi was the least attractive of the bunch. She had a buck-toothed smile and lanky legs. Iris Introduced Mariana and I to her friends. Yaya gave a scornful look as she squeezed my hand. A faint scent of marijuana touched my nose as Naomi greeted me. The ladies ordered their first round of drinks. I didn't want to be included in their girl talk, so I turned my attention to the television. The Florida State Seminoles were playing against The Syracuse Orange. Yaya poked my shoulder.

"Why do guys do that, Price?" she

asked. I turned to her. "Do what?"

"Screw our brains out and say, 'let's keep it casual.' It's ridiculous."

"Men will cuddle, fuck you raw, and tell you his dreams, then tell us not to catch feelings," Naomi added.

"Men do nothing but waste our time," Mariana yelled over the loud music.

"Women do the same thing," I answered.

"Fuck outta here," Iris said.

"If I had a nickel for every time a woman has wasted my time, I'd have enough to buy a soda," I said.

"How do we waste a man's time?" Iris asked.

"Oh, you don't know, Iris? You don't how you waste a man's time?" I softly smacked the table.

"Women have mastered the art of wasting a man's time. They will lead a man on, accept his date offers, entertain his feelings, and use him for his companionship, while waiting for the guy she really wants to get his act together. Women use the friend zone to their advantage. They pretend to be into a guy they have no interest in when they're lonely. Instead of being honest with their intentions, they deceive the good guys.

"Men are scumbags, but at least we're upfront about it. When I want to be with a woman, I tell her. When I want to have sex, I show her nothing more."

"There should be a way both parties can express their intentions without confusing the other," Yaya said.

"There is. It's called telling the truth," I answered.

The conversation was getting too intense, so I stepped out for a smoke. Naomi followed soon after. She babbled about the friend zone conversation. A migraine pounded my head, so I politely asked her to shut up. I followed her to her car to smoke a joint. Her interior reeked of strong smell.

"Can you explain your comments back at the bar?" She passed the joint. I took a few puffs.

"Both men and women suck at relationships because we don't know what we want. We just fuck and fuck until someone gets hurt. We get so fixated on not getting hurt we forget to be vulnerable. Without it we're lost souls, aimlessly wandering while breaking the hearts of many along the way." I passed the joint.

"I'm mad you held the joint for so long, but beautiful rant, though."

We finished the joint. She received a call from Iris who was ready to go home and needed me to drive. Naomi drove to the parking lot Iris was located at. Iris was slouched in the passenger's seat and Mariana was curled in the back seat.

I got out of Naomi's car and got in the driver's seat of the other car. I smoked a cigarette to calm my anxiety. Iris turned to me and smiled. I started the car and drove. The speedometer remained under 30 mph. The traffic was light and there were no cops in sight. Thank God, because I didn't want to die.

Iris was stable enough to walk on her own. I lifted Mariana by her rear and carried her inside. I placed Mariana on the couch as Iris stumbled to her room. I fixed a cup of instant tea then took it to Iris' room. She was lying face down on her blanket sobbing. She wore only a black bra with matching lace panties.

"Sorry. I'll come back later," I said.

She turned over. "You can come in," she said.

I entered the room, placed the cup of tea on her nightstand and sat next to her.

"What's wrong?"

"Ramone forgot my birthday."

"What?" I responded. "He could have got his days mixed up. It happens." I handed her the tea.

"Why are you defending him?" She sipped the tea then placed the cup back on the nightstand.

I shrugged. "I don't know."

"He can be an ass at times."

"All men are, including me. It's all about finding the asshole you can tolerate the most."

"You always knew how to make me laugh." She sipped the tea again before placing it down.

"I never thanked you for saving my life," I said.

101

"Oh, it was nothing," she nudged me. We laughed until we locked eyes. The stare lasted longer than usual. I went in for a kiss and she met me halfway. I groped her breasts as our lips intertwined. My hand went to rubbing her clit. She gasped and pushed me away.

"What the hell are you doing?" she asked.

"Kissing you."

"Keep doing it." She mounted me.

I kicked my pants off while she sucked my neck. She slides her panties to the side and rode my shaft in a circular motion. Her body quivered as I teased her nipples with my tongue.

She laughed. "Are you moaning?"

"Of course," I answered.

"So hot." Her pussy became wetter and wetter.

We switched positions. I stared into her eyes passionately as I stroked inside of her with deep slow strokes, I wanted her to fall in love. She sunk her teeth into my nipple. I grimaced but didn't make a sound. Her teeth nearly ripped through my flesh, and the pain felt good. She continued biting and back scratching until we climaxed together.

I rolled over to the other side of the bed.

"That was amazing!" she exclaimed. "I

know. I was there," I smirked.

We stared at the cycling ceiling fan in silence, trying to avoid the obvious conversation. She curled in the sheets. I got dressed and tiptoed out the room.

I overheard Mariana puking in the bathroom. I fixed a glass of water and took it to her. I pulled her hair as she hurled Patron and pizza clumps. The smell was so putrid I almost puked. She flushed the vomit then sat on the toilet.

"Do you love Iris?" she asked. "Where

the hell is this coming from?"

"The way you look at her. The way she makes you laugh. And the way you refuse to speak to me when she's around." She sipped some of the water I'd given her. "It's obvious."

I nodded. "It sucks because I'll never have her."

"True."

"What should I do?"

"Forget about it and find someone else to love."

"It's not easy." I gave her a hug and went to my room.

I streamed Marvin Gaye's, *I Want You* via Spotify and began writing. I craved a drink. Writing while sober didn't feel natural. Booze had been my fuel. It had given me the courage to be honest. Without liquor, I believed my writing was as dull as sex between two Amish people.

Iris entered the room and sat on the edge of the bed. She was silent as I typed. Sometimes silence can speak a thousand words. We were too stubborn to speak, but we knew what we needed to say. She would clear her throat, and I would look over my shoulder, and the words remained silent.

"What are you doing in here...in the dark...with him?" Mariana entered the room. "Nothing, we were just talking," Iris said.

"Yeah, talking." I smiled at Iris.

"What's got you up?" Iris asked.

"This stomach ache and your smelly couch," Mariana answered.

"I told Ramone to stop sitting on the couch naked," Iris said.

"Ew." Mariana grimaced.

"Nothing wrong with going commando," I giggle.

Iris and Mariana got in my bed and snuggled under the sheets. I wrote until slivers of daylight seeped through the window blinds. I had a gut feeling something strange was about to happen. My eyes did not rest at all.

GOD IS A WOMAN

RUNNIN' ON EMPTY

Two weeks later, I was healthier than ever. I was doing yoga twice a week, lifting weights three days a week, and thanks to Iris, I'd finally acquired my drivers' license. My job as a tutor was going well. Teaching children how to read and write filled a void. What I loved the most about children was how genuine they were. Kids didn't care about what you possessed or who you were; they only cared about your heart. They remained pure, until life ate at their innocent souls; forcing them to turn cold and shallow as they grow old. Life fucks us all.

I arrived at Iris' place during the early evening. Ramone was expected to arrive the next morning, and I had to gather my belongings.

Iris was cleaning the house with *Easter Pink* by Future rattling through the sound system. Iris' taste in music was profound. She could go from Fleetwood Mac to Gucci Mane at the drop of a dime. Gotta love a woman with balance.

Since our night of passionate lovemaking, we agreed it was a one-time deal. We were both vulnerable and the situation should never be mentioned again.

I looked at her butt as she vacuumed in tight PINK brand shorts. I saw the folds between her brows as she pushed the vacuum with extra force.

"What's wrong?" I yelled over the noise. She didn't hear me, so I yelled again and again and again. Finally, I unplugged the vacuum and muted the music.

"What's wrong? You look pissed."

"Ramone called and said he has to stay in Atlanta for two more weeks," she huffed.

"Okay. Let's go to Disney

World." "What?"

"Are you deaf? I said, let's go to Disney World."

"What a great idea!" She hopped into my arms. "Let's go!"

I wanted to do something to show my gratification for everything she had done for me. I also wanted her to get her mind off Ramone. Her head was spinning over him. He was brief when they conversed and would rarely call her.

We hit the road thirty minutes later. She assumed the driving responsibility as I played the DJ. She was in a cheerful mood and laughed at my corny jokes and sang along to the music. She had a raspy yet angelic voice. We sang together when "Show You the Way to Go" by The Jacksons played. She was the only person who loved Michael Jackson as much as I did.

"Are you still marrying

him?" "Of course, Why?"

"Because we're obviously supposed to be together," I said.

"We'll never be more than friends."

"How could you say that after you had my penis inside of you?"

"How romantic. For a writer, you have such a shitty way with words."

I laughed until I looked at her pouty face. For the rest of the ride we were silent. We would occasionally sing-along to Lil Wayne or Michael Jackson lyrics as their songs played, but that's it. When I looked at her, she kept her eyes locked on the road.

The bright lights of the magical park lit the skyline. The weather dropped as we waited in line for our tickets. I gave her my cardigan to wear but her upper lip remained stiff.

"Are you still mad at me?"

"No."

"What is it?"

"Ramone. I checked his credit card statement and I think he's cheating," she said. "His purchases were typical, but he's paying for two every time."

"You can tell he ain't a player." I laughed. "Real players have secret credit cards so they can cheat in peace."

"If we were to ever date, I'm holding your wallet," she snapped.

"You already have it."

"Real funny." She shook her head.

"Do I See a smile?"

We ambled through the park and admired its mystic. The fall sky contrasted with the theme park lights and created a beautiful atmosphere. I ate churros and she munched on a pretzel. We boarded the Buzz Lightyear's Space Ranger Spin and the Astro Orbiter.

As we stood in line for hotdogs, Iris noticed a guy from afar. She thought he was Ramone and I assumed it was a random guy in nut-compressing jeans. His jeans were tighter than a poor man's budget. I tried to make out his face, but the lights glared off his sunglasses. When he turned to his date I took the opportunity get a closer look.

"What the hell?" I yelled. Ramone looked over his shoulder.

"Hey buddy, how are ya?" I greeted.

"The writer guy. Show me some love." He hugged me. "What are you doing here?"

"I'm basking in the ambiance." I whiffed the air. "Who's the beautiful gal?"

He looked at me then looked at her. "She's my sister." His eyes widened, and I turned around to see why. Iris was rushing towards us with a large cup of soda. I stepped to the side. Soda and ice shot in midair faster than a blink of an eye.

"You son of a bitch," she screamed. Ramone dodged to the left. "No," Iris yelled.

The contents splashed all over my vintage Michael Jackson *Beat It* shirt.

"Seriously, how could you miss him?" I asked. I was infuriated. That shirt was one of the few gifts I'd ever received from my mother, and it was a rare collectible.

110

For a moment, Iris stood without a single movement. She didn't flinch, blink or breathe. She stared at the shameful face of her fiancé. Ramone tried to speak, but the words weren't coming out. Iris started crying and stormed away.

I went after Iris. I found her sitting at a table with her face rested on her palm. Her eyes were listless as she gazed into the distance. I offered her a cigarette. She took my last two and snapped them in half.

"I know you're mad about spilling Coke all over my rare collectible tee shirt, but it's just a shirt. It's okay." I rubbed her back.

"You're such an idiot." She laughed. "Let's get out of here."

"Okay."

I got behind the wheel on the way back home. Iris had one leg resting on the dashboard with the seat reclined. People were driving like their heads were cut off. I began to maneuver through traffic in a timid manner. Come to Daddy by R Kelly started to play. I kept my focus on the road with a devilish grin on my face.

"Wipe the smirk off your face," Iris said.

"Why? I love this song." I continued to sing. "Come to Daddy. Let me please your

111

body tonight." She shook her head and smiled. We ran into a harsh downpour when we crossed the Skyway Bridge. I was too uneasy to continue driving and stopped at the Waffle House.

"You two make such a pretty couple," The server greeted as we entered.
"Er," Iris said.
"Thank you," I exclaimed.

Iris ordered coffee and a pecan waffle. I ordered water and a bacon Angus cheeseburger. Her phone was buzzing uncontrollably on the table. Ramone called and texted until her battery drained. Her words came few and far in between during our sitting. She ate a small portion of her waffle and barely sipped her coffee.

"Ramone's been screwing around since we've been together." She sipped her coffee. "I thought I could deal with it, because all men cheat."

"That's the dumbest shit I've ever heard." I shook my head.

The rain began to settle, so we got back on the road. The smooth tunes of Boney James created a peaceful vibe during the ride. Iris asked to shack up at my house until she found another place to stay.

Going back to the place that had ruined me felt like I was going back to a dark hole, but this time I had an angel with me. We made a quick stop to her condo to gather our belongings then went to my house.

My lawn was crowded with trash and newspapers were piled at the front door. A strong stench punched us in the nose when we opened the door. It smelt like a dead dog. Glass was shattered under a broken living room window. The television was missing. I ran to my room and noticed my television, stereo, and Xbox 360 were gone. Dirty dishes were piled in the sink and the trashcan overflowed to the floor. The broken fridge contained moldy leftovers and a bottle of gin. Iris took a shot and poured it down the drain. The electricity was still on, thankfully.

I emptied the trashcans and dumped the dirty dishes. Scrubbing them would have been pointless. We scrubbed and cleaned until the odor was bearable.

For the rest of the night, we listened to music, and I taught her how to play chess. For the first time in ten years, a slight rush of happiness made my heart beat. Iris' presence brought more joy than any amount of alcohol or pussy. I didn't mind being sober around her. I no longer felt empty. Thanks to her, I wanted to be alive again.

JOY TO THE WORLD

Christmas was approaching, and the temperature dropped to the mid 60's. Finally, a winter in Florida. I could see my breath in the air, and for the first time in years I could wear sweaters without people asking, "Aren't you hot?". Iris decorated the tree with ornaments and hung the lights outside. My siblings were visiting, and I tried to make it their best holiday season ever.

Things between Iris and I were going well. She finally gave in and decided to love me. I was in bliss. I even stopped smoking because the smell of cigarettes turned her off. I finished writing my first screenplay and began writing a new novel, *For You, I'll Die,* and I was in the best shape of my life.

Iris answered a phone call. It was Mariana. They chatted for a few minutes. "Okay I'll text you my new address. Can't wait to see you," Iris said as she concluded the conversation.

My eyes lit up when she said, "My new address."

She told me Mariana had some big news she wanted to tell us. It was odd she hadn't said it over the phone.

114

She laughed and went to the door. My siblings hugged Iris then trotted to me. They appeared to be happier than ever. Jordan had a new haircut and his acne scars were cleared. Thomas and Frankie walked in carrying their luggage. I complimented Jordan's fresh look as well as poked fun at his new gut. Thomas and Frankie were feeding them well. I introduced Iris to Thomas and Frankie. They marveled at her grace and beauty. Thomas took one look around and noticed the board covering the broken window.

"My God, did someone break in here?" he asked.

"Yup. And took the TVs," Iris responded.

"I'll buy you one for Christmas," he offered.

"It's cool. I don't care for TV anymore," I said.

Later that evening, we visited Kresge House Christmas lights display. It's an illustrious display of Christmas lights in the form of a maze for families to explore and enjoy various actives. It's a hometown tradition three decades long.

I held Ashlyn in my arm as I held Iris' hand. Life felt perfect. Iris eventually took Ashlyn and Jordan and Frankie followed her. I was left alone with Thomas.

"You look happy," Thomas said.

"Thanks to her," I answered.

"I can tell. Your posture is straight, clothes ironed, and your amazing smile is showing. I'm happy for you."

"She saved my life."
"She's beautiful."
"No, she literally saved my life," I said.
"Wait, what?"
"I tried to off myself, but she found me."
"Dammit, I told you if you ever needed anything to contact me."

"During that time, no one could've saved me not even God."

"Jesus, Price." He patted me on the

back." "That has a nice ring to it."

Thomas smiled with those huge teeth and I no longer saw a molester, abuser, or drug addict. I saw a man who'd found peace and one who had made amends. My wounds were healed, but the scars remained visible. I had

117

forgiven Thomas, and I was in a better place for it.

Later, Iris and I were cuddled under the sheets. I played with her clit from behind and whispered sweet nothings in her ear. It felt great to be in love again, real love. The worst part of loving someone is knowing you're going to lose them one day through death or disappointment, and all we can do is enjoy the moment.

Iris smelt so sweet. She always did. I held her like she was all I had. I buried my face in her curly wild hair. It was my safe place.

"Babe?" she said.
"Yes?"
"How far do you see us going?"
"My only concern is this moment right now. The future is not guaranteed so why care?"

Jordan entered the room and flipped the light switch.

"Turn the light off."

"Someone's here to see you," he said. Mariana followed him. Her face was bare, and her hair was tied in a ponytail. She wore some large hoodie and blue sweatpants. She appeared to be baffled at the sight of us half naked and cuddled together. Jordan left the room.

We got dressed as her large deep brown eyes stared at us with disappointment.

"Want anything to drink?" Iris asked.

"I would like to know what the hell is going on?" Mariana responded.

"We're dating," I said.

"Well, good for you because, I'm pregnant." She scowled. She crossed her arms. My heart skipped a few beats, and the sounds of the world become muted.

"Oh, my God, congrats, baby. Who's the lucky guy?" Iris asked.

I looked at my feet, at the ceiling, and over at the walls. The room became soundless. Iris stared into Marina's misty eyes then her eyes locked eyes with mine for a moment. I shook my head.

"No. No. No. No. No," she wailed.

"Babe, listen," I said.

She covered her mouth and stormed out the room. Moments later, we found Iris on the bathroom floor throwing up in the toilet. I held her hair back. She was hysterical. I tried to explain, but I couldn't get a sentence in. She

119

cried, cursed, and hurled at the same time. Iris cleaned herself and we went out to the patio.

I told her about the one-night stand I'd had with Mariana. She was broken and so was I. To disappoint the one, you love is one of the worst feelings in the world.

Mariana mentioned the baby could be her ex-boyfriend's. She wasn't sure, but she'd felt like she needed to tell me.

I took a seat. I longed for some smokes and a cold six packs. My heart was throbbing so hard it almost ripped through my chest. I sat there shaking and rocking.

Iris spent the next ten minutes comforting Mariana. Mariana eventually drove off. I looked to Iris. She sat stone-faced as her nostrils flared. A thousand apologies would not mend our broken bond.

I'd felt it instantly, Iris slipping away from me.

"Fuck you," she hissed and slapped my cheek.

"I deserved that."

She continued to wail on me. I hunched over and shielded my face. She punched my back as if she was in a sparring match.

"You piece of shit." She slapped my head.

120

"I can't believe I trusted you."

I took the beating until she stopped to catch her breath. I had nothing to say. I looked at her red puffy face. She gave my face a good opened-hand slap and went inside.

Blood dripped from my lip. She came back out with her purse hanging from her shoulder and stormed to her car. I stared at the tire marks she left as she reversed out of the driveway.

I went inside to look for my wallet. Everyone was upstairs sleeping.

"She still has it," I said.

My call went to voicemail a dozen times. I texted her.

Can I get my wallet?

You're so fucking weak. You think booze will solve all your problems, she replied. **"Yes, or nah?"** She left no response.

Sore and sober, I sat in the dark. An unsettling sensation erupted in my gut. I knew she was gone, for good. My brief stint of happiness hand came crumbling because of a quick fuck. And a quick fuck had turned into a maybe baby.

Since I didn't have my ID, I went to the only spot in town that didn't have the morals to card me, Bottoms up Gentleman's Club. It was on the darker side of town. My neighborhood was white family friendly compared to that area, but I needed to be surrounded by tits and low standards.

A strong draft of heat suffocated me as I entered the joint. Some lights were dimmed, some lights flickered between bright and dull. Seven other patrons were sitting by the stage idly watching Sharli the pregnant stripper. The horny men cheered and threw dollar bills at the soon to be mother. I sat at the bar and asked for a double shot of Hennessy, no chasers, no cubes. The server was a classmate of mine. She appeared to be dejected and worn out. She'd gained a lot of girth since our school days. Her eyes were wearied with heavy circles underneath them.

"Remember me, Prom Queen? "I asked.

"How could I forget the guy who got caught jerking off in the bathroom?" she said and smirked.

"Yup, my claim to fame. How's life?" I sipped my drink

"You see where I'm at." She shrugged.

"I'm with ya. We're in one hell of a paradise."

"I see you're a writer now. We always knew you were going to do extraordinary things. You were too dorky not too."

"Thank you."

I ordered another drink and watched two gentlemen squabble by the stage. The bouncer, a six-foot eight vascular white male, dragged the drunken buffoons across the floor until he tossed them out like Thanksgiving leftovers.

The back of my shirt was damped with sweat. A soft hand caressed my inner thigh.

"Hey, handsome. I'm Reina."

I looked over my shoulder. A woman of decent height and fair skin smiled at me. Her bra was hanging by a thread trying to contain those massive breasts. Her ass was full and much bigger than what I was used to handling. She rubbed her knee into my groin.

"You smell surprisingly pleasant," I said.

"Thanks. I'm fresh out the shower. Wanna take this to the back, so I can dry you off?" I answered. She took my hand.

"Take care of my baby sister, alright?" the bartender said.

The private room smelt like a group of monkeys had an orgy. Reina took off my shirt and handed me a towel. She straddled my lap and started grinding. I grabbed her ass. I began to sweat more, but she wasn't sweating. She must've been immune to the club's heat.

"Guys like you don't come here often," she said.

"Like me?"

"Yeah, young, good looking, not bald."

"But I'm also a piece of shit, but I mean well."

She smothered my face with her sopping breasts. I licked her erect nipples.

"You're far too pretty to work here," I said.

"Exactly, there's no competition. Guys are more likely to ask for me."

"Smart business girl."

She felt my erection bulging through my sweatpants. She grasped it firmly. I grabbed her hand, but I couldn't resist the temptation. The carnal side of me wasn't ready to change.

"For sixty dollars, I'll relieve this for

you." "Deal."

124

She pulled my penis out sucked for a few minutes.

"Turn around," I demanded.

She positioned herself on all fours. Her backside was plump and pretty with stretch marks on the cheeks. I'd always loved stretch marks; they resembled naturalness.

I fucked her hard and with no finesse. I treated her like the slut she was and came all over her back.

"What the heck, dude?"

"What?"

"On my back? Really?"

"Where else was I supposed to aim?"

"The towel, the chair, the floor, anywhere, but my body."

"Whatever. Thanks for the nut." I gave her the money, purchased another drink and left the club.

I drove to Iris' condo hoping she would be there. I banged on the door. "Iris." I continued to knock. "Baby, open up."

"Yo, shut the fuck up. I'm trying to sleep," her neighbor yelled.

"How about you shut the fu-" I stopped mid-sentence when caught a glimpse of the tall, heavy set man. "I'll tone it down a bit. Sorry."

He went back inside. The door opened, but instead of seeing Iris, I was face-to-face with Ramone. He wore a robe and smoked a cigar. I chuckled. His face was stern. I caught a swift right hook to the jaw. I stumbled over my foot and used his body to break my fall. He connected again with an uppercut. I was out for the count. My body twitched on the tile.

"You son of a bitch." He kicked my stomach as if he was punting a football. The oxygen from my lungs left my soul. He continued to stomp my ribs, stomach, and chest, with his hard-bottomed Stacey Adams. Why was he wearing those shoes at two in the morning?

Blood and Hennessy were the only tastes lingering in my mouth. A wad of spit landed on my forehead followed by the sound of Ramone slamming the door.

I stood to my feet with blood oozing from my mouth. I bumped into the walls as I hobbled the hallway. A tenant rushed to aid me.

"Oh my god, what happened?" she asked.

"I fell. Don't worry about me."

"We need to get you to the hospital."

"I'm fine. Please, leave me alone." I tripped and suddenly my forehead clashed with the hallway. I lost consciousness. In twenty-four hours, my life had reverted to the misery of which I was accustomed to.

I knew happiness was nothing but a fool's gold. A guy like me didn't deserve to be happy.

GOD IS A WOMAN

MERRY FUCKING CHRISTMAS

It was Christmas morning and I was ailing in a hospital bed. Jordan was bedside catering to my needs. Thomas and Frankie were singing carols to Ashlyn. They sounded terrible, but Ash seemed to be enjoying herself.

Doctor Grier walked in holding a clipboard.

"What's the diagnosis, Doc?" I asked.

"You have a few cracked ribs, internal bleeding, and a concussion. You took quite a beating, Price."

"It tends to happen when you screw a guy's fiancé and impregnate his sister."

His eyebrows lifted. "Sounds like a Tyler Perry film."

"Trust me, it's way better than any film Tyler Perry has ever made."

He laughed and left the room.

I told my family they could leave and enjoy Christmas without me.

For the next few hours, I wrote. I was almost finished with my forthcoming novel and I was optimistic,

Iris came to visit, which soothed my soul. She wore a hoodie and a pair of shades. Her hair covered her cheeks.

"Price, thank God you're okay." She gave a hug and a kiss.

"Are you okay?" I asked.

"Sure. Why?" She flinched as I reached for the shades.

"He hit you, too, didn't he?" She nodded. "If I could, I would kick his ass," I said. Her eyes rolled. "I'm sure you would." "I love you," I said.

"You're cool." She smiled.

"Do you forgive me?" I asked.

"No. You got another woman pregnant."

"Allegedly."

"Whatever the case. We can't be together. Not now, at least."

"I understand."

129

I checked out early because I hated everything about hospitals: the beds, the temperature check, the needles, and IVs; being there made me wish I was dead.

Iris drove me home so I could spend Christmas with my family, but she didn't stay.

Later, I went to an open mic event. The crowd was intimate. I took a seat next to a pale tattooed woman. She gave a warm smile and introduced herself. Her name was Karen. She was frail with a nice sized rack.

"Can I bum a smoke?" I asked.

"Sure."

I put the square to my lip and she lit it. Being surrounded by carefree life-goers and poets created a lively atmosphere. I felt unbothered.

"Do you write?" Karen asked.

"Yeah, but spoken word isn't my thing."

"Be cool and get up there."

"Nah."

"Hey, we have a new talent, right here," she yelled. The host invited me to the stage, but I declined. "Get on stage, get on stage." Karen chanted.

130

"Alright. I'll do it but if I suck it's your fault." I approached the stage.

"What's your name young man?" The host asked.

"Price Jones."

"Give a warm welcome to Mr. Price Jones," he told the crowd who applauded in response.

I got stunned by a bright spotlight. My heart pounded as if someone was holding a gun to my head. My left leg shivered when I grabbed the mic stand.

"Hey, I'm Price and I'm going to recite something I wrote the other day. It's called, *"Ax of Life."*

All the women glanced and smirked. The room was warm and quiet as all eyes were glued to me. I tapped the ashes from my cigarette, and I shut my eyes tight.

Life is an ax it chops you

Piece by piece

Until your flesh and bones

Are obsolete

You scream and weep

To stop the pain

Then your blood is splattered

131

And washed by rain

You pray to be saved

But no one answers your call

It's not until the ax hits your final limb

You realize you're all alone

That's why I love drugs and the numbness

So, when the ax comes

I won't feel it at all

I opened my eyes to a crowd of cheerful faces and wide eyes. My heart settled. I wiped the sweat from my forehead and walked off stage.

"The hell you doing man? Keep going," a gentleman in the crowd yelled.

The small crowd began to clamor for an encore. I trotted back on stage and recited another poem. Then another poem. And another. I had the crowd at my fingertips. They were mesmerized. The feeling was empowering. I had never known I had the ability to touch people in such a way.

I took my seat next to Karen. She gazed at me with her flirtatious eyes. She lit another smoke and handed it to me. A short gentleman took a seat in front of me. He wore a tight blue suit and his cologne smelt phenomenal. He turned to me.

"Hey, good show tonight." We shook hands. "I'm Marty Waters."

"Cool name."

"Thanks. Are you seeking management?"

"Not really."

"Well, if you ever change your mind, give me a ring." He handed me a business card.

I excused myself to go to the restroom. My pants were to my knees before I made it to a stall. At first, I struggled to release. After a third attempt urine blasted out faster than a fire hose. My dick felt like I was pissing a flame. "Fuck." I shrieked. I fell to my knees and sobbed as the piss continued to flow. The agony grew worse until it stopped. I squirmed on that filthy floor with my dick cuffed in my palms.

"Ha, you got burnt," a gentleman in the next stall said.

I was mortified. Years of having unprotected sex had finally caught up with me. In one week, I'd discovered I was having a child and contracted an STD. And I'd lost Iris because of it. My reckless behavior was the reason behind my miserable life. Not my

133

childhood, not the women, and not alcohol. It was me. And nothing was going to change unless I stopped blaming everyone else.

GOD IS A WOMAN

THE VISIT TO THE ABORTION CLINIC

The next morning, I left the health clinic with a sore arm and feeling light-headed. I'd nearly fainted when the syringe needle pierced through my skin. I'd never liked taking shots. They always reminded me of my mother shooting up. I was told the gonorrhea would clear once the antibodies finish their job.

A light drizzle rained from the sky. The cold droplets felt refreshing as they showered my skin. Mariana called. She wanted me to come to the abortion clinic with her in Clearwater. I reluctantly agreed. I wasn't thrilled about having a child, but killing one was something I'd never condoned. When you make your bed, you must lay in it. Our one-night stand had been a mistake, and we had to own up to the consequences.

Her black Honda Civic pulled in the driveway two hours later. Our words were minimal, and the silence was strong. We hardly looked at each other. She wore on oversized Dallas Cowboys hoodie and no makeup, baring the dark rings under her eyes.

"Did you get any sleep last night?" I asked.

She kept her focus on the road and didn't say a word. The radio was broken so we sat in silence along with our thoughts.

I reminisced about the time Iris told me she'd gone through with the procedure. She wasn't the same to me. We weren't the same. It had ripped a small hole into me knowing what she had done.

I wanted to tell Mariana to have the baby, but as a man, I had no right to tell a woman what to do with her body. Besides, the unborn baby was the lucky one. What if not being born was better than living all together? Bringing a child into this world would be pure torture, especially being black and poor. No one deserved to be black and poor in America.

The drive lasted twenty minutes. The parking lot was nearly filled. Mariana's sandals scratched against the gravel as she trudged her way inside. I stayed in the car to burn a cigarette. My heart rattled as the smoke hit my lungs. The drizzle began to cry sideways as the gale was carrying it. Hearing the raindrops hit the windshield was therapeutic. I reclined and listened to the rainfall.

136

I called Iris to tell her I loved her. She didn't need to say it back. I heard her smile through the phone.

I got out the car and went inside the clinic. Mariana was seated in the fetal position with fear on her face. I went to her and rubbed her back. The wait was long, too long. And the office was toasty. The song *Daughters* by John Mayer played over the intercom. It was a bit insensitive, but I guess they couldn't control what the radio played.

All the patients appeared gloomy and unwilling. When their name got called, they had tears in their eyes or wore shades to conceal their face. My heart goes out any woman who had to make that decision. It was a heavy weight to carry alone. Women are the strongest beings on earth. They can withstand anything.

After a two hour wait, Mariana's name was called. I stood with her. She placed her head on my chest. I planted a kiss on her forehead. I watched her walk slowly to the abortionist. I gazed around the room and saw all the women giving me scolding stares. I sat and hid behind an Ebony magazine.

Ten minutes later, Mariana came running from behind the door. She fell to her knees and sobbed in her palms.

137

"Mari, what's wrong?" I rushed to her.

"I can't do it. I can't do it. I can't do it," she wept.

"Come on. Let's go. We'll talk in the car." I tried to get her up.

"I saw a dead baby," she said tonelessly. I picked her up and carried her outside to the car. The drizzle was gone, but the wind was still heavy and humid.

I took the wheel. Mari could settle her flustered emotions a bit. She was shaken. She described the horrid scene she saw. She'd heard the cries of a heartbroken would-have been mother and saw the crushed skull and broken limbs of an unborn fetus as the doctor leisurely carried it away.

"Price, I'm sorry. I couldn't kill a baby."

"Don't be sorry. You know I'm here for you."

"What about Iris?"

"Don't worry 'bout her. We'll get through it."

On the ride, back we conversed more. She seemed at ease with her decision. I knew I wasn't ready to be a parent, but a person is never prepared to be responsible for another life We're all fucked up, but sometimes a person becomes more rational, responsible and happier when a child enters their life.

Even though I was piss poor, I had a lot of love to give, and my child was going to have an endless supply of it.

I drove Mariana home then hopped on the bus and got off at the nearest stop to Somethin' Different. It was early afternoon and I was already thinking about getting faded. Before I could order a drink, I heard a voice calling my name. It was Iris.

"I saw you walking here. What the hell are you doing?" She twisted my ear. I winced.

"I'm about to drink until I'm numb." I tried to pull away, but the pain worsened.

"Oh no you're not." She dragged me out of the bar and embarrassed me like she was my mother.

She took the box of cigarettes from my shirt pocket and tossed it into the road. I was so pissed. Iris always showed tough love, the kind of love I needed the most. She wanted to see me be great even when I had no belief in myself.

We went to Sushi Inc. for lunch. I was quiet at the table, and she began to suspect something was wrong with me.

"Are you okay over there?" she asked.

"I'm fine." I shook my head.

"When I see you, sad boy face I know something's wrong."

"It's just..." I hesitated.

"Talk to me."

"Mari and I went to the abortion clinic," I said.

She stared at me with disgust. She attempted to leave the table, but I grabbed her arm.

"How could you?" she whispered.

"We didn't do it. She couldn't do it."

"Good, because it was the biggest mistake of my life." She sat. "I still wake up in tears from the nightmares I have because I killed my child." A teardrop rolled from her left eye. She'd lived in regret for years wondering what could have been.

We spend most of our lives pondering the plethora of 'what ifs' that may drain our happiness. Dwelling does nothing but waste time. Life has no mulligans. We must move forward and pray. Pain and regret play an interesting role in our lives. If we succumb to it, we become timid, but if we prevail, the possibilities are endless.

140

After lunch, we went back to the Tradewinds Beach Resorts, where she was staying for the week. She had a beach view room. We sat on the balcony to watch the low tides splash along the coast. She sipped wine, and I sipped tea.

"I meant to mention this before, but I like the new hair," I complimented.

She smiled. "I like how you always notice."

"How could I not?"

Her dimple showed as she smirked.

Her hair was straightened and dyed chestnut brown, and it looked lovely on her. She had something on her mind and I could tell. Iris would usually bite her bottom lip and gaze at the sky when she was in deep thought.

"Price, I don't know how to tell you this." "Gosh, are you pregnant, too?"

"Hell no, idiot."

I blew a sigh of relief and she rolled her eyes.

"I got accepted to become Dean of Admissions at UCLA."

"Great!" I hugged her.

"I leave right after New Year's."

141

It felt like my breath got sucked right out. I tried to find the right words to say, but nothing came out.

Iris went back inside. I patted my pockets and remembered she'd thrown my smokes away. My arms shook. I needed something to calm my nerves. I stormed through the room.

"Price, where are you going?" she asked, as I headed for the door. I remained silent.

"For a drink." I grabbed the doorknob.

"The hell you're not." She rushed from the bed to stop me. She grabbed my arm, but I snatched it away.

"How could you do this to me?"

"Do what?" She reached for me.

"You storm back into my life, then you leave. You can't keep doing this shit to me. I can't lose you again."

"I'm sorry, but I have to do this. Besides, you're having a baby and I can't be a part of that." Her eyes became misty.

"It may not be mine," I reminded her.

"Either way, I gotta leave." I drew her closer to me. She put her hands in mine.

I winced as my upper arm grazed the wall. Iris gave a suspicious look. I tried to play it off,

142

but Iris was too smart of a woman. She stepped away.

"What's going on?"

"Nothing."

She pinched my sore area. I gasped. She lifted my sleeve and saw the circular Band-Aid covering the sore spot.

"This is nothing, I got a vaccine today."

"You're such a fucking liar. There are two things I know about you. You hate doctors and you hate shots," she shouted.

I kept denying, but she refused to believe me.

"You got burned, didn't you?"

I nodded with my face down. I couldn't look at her. I saw her feet stomping their way to the bed. I lumbered out the room, but shut the door gently. I walked the hallway and broke down to my knees. Once again, my lack of self-control had gotten me back at ground zero.

My face became wet from my sobbing. A wandering girl approached me. She was the cutest little girl. She was no older than seven.

She offered me some Skittles, so I held my hand out. Her mother came calling for her.

143

"What have I told you about talking to strangers, Ashanti?" The mother said while grabbing her daughter. "No offense," she told me.

"None taken," I responded.

"But he was crying," the little girl said.

"You have a beautiful daughter." I wiped my eyes.

"Thank you. And remember, if it doesn't kill you, you've won the battle."

She and her daughter seemingly vanished. She'd been a pretty woman too. The kind of beauty you would find in a vintage magazine. She was like an angel who'd given me priceless advice. She's shone like a rainbow through the dark cloud of my dismal day.

I rushed to Iris' and banged on the door until she answered. I grabbed her and ran my hands through her hair. She was so warm. She wrapped her arms around me. I kissed her forehead, cheek, and neck.

"Please forgive me," I begged. "I can't lose you." She nodded and stared into my eyes. She knew her glare was my weakness. Her eyes were my haven. "You saved my life, and I have to prove it wasn't a mistake."

144

"Stop talking crazy. I would have saved you even if I didn't know you."

"That's why you're a special woman."

"I know. I'm frigging amazing." She laughed.

We spent the rest of the day frolicking at the resort. We played mini golf and grubbed on some good seafood and sang karaoke.

Iris loved to sing. And I loved hearing her voice even more. She reminded me of my mother when she'd sung in the church choir. I'd been a child, but those memories were still vivid.

We checked out and went to my place. Having her in my bed again made me feel safe. Iris was an angel and in my bed, was where she needed to be. I felt half empty without her. She was strong enough to forgive me for my nonsense, and I owed her the world for it.

She slept peacefully. She was curled with her hands placed under her face. "Your face is the face I wanna wake up to for the rest of my life," I whispered as I watched her sleep.

I shook her shoulder until she snapped out her dream.

"What do you want?" she asked with her groggy voice.

"I'm going with you," I said.

She rubbed her eyes. "Wait…you can't. You're having a baby."

"If it's mine, I'll come back, but I have to go for my career. There's nothing here for me."

"You're right. You're far too talented for this small city. It's time to spread your wings and fly."

"And thanks to you, I will."

She smiled. "Good night, love."

"Night, babe."

I raised to my feet and walked into the living room, so I could write without interrupting her rest. I completed the first draft of my novel and two television pilots. Iris had no clue how much she inspired me.

After three in the morning, I went back to bed and rested next to the love of my life.

THE FLIGHT

On New Year's Day, Iris and I boarded the flight. We figured it made no sense to wait an extra day to change our lives. I yearned for a

146

cigarette more than ever. When the plane left the ground, my heart began to pound through my shirt, and I was short of breath. Iris laughed, but she held my hand. It was my first flight, and the first time moving out of my hometown. Being afraid was natural when dealing with the unfamiliar. I gazed at the pillow shaped clouds and saw the earth from a bird's point of view and realized how insignificant I was, how irrelevant we all were.

When it's all said and done, everything we've stressed about and all we've worked for will vanish, and the world will continue without us.

'Don't worry, babe, you're gonna be great in Cali. You deserve this." Iris rested her head on my shoulder. She had a unique way of making me believe everything was going to be okay. Her voice was so soft and reassuring. Her words were like gospel to me.

It's funny how life works. One minute, I was sulking in my own misery, the next I was on a plane with the love of my life ready to embark on new possibilities and start a new life.

Love is a funny thing, too. When I hated myself, when I believed I was a failure, when I'd lost all hope in love and aspirations, and when I'd believed I was going to die in some

147

random pussy or choking on my own vomit, she'd come out of nowhere and had shown me how to love again.

The feeling she brought to me was indescribable. She made me feel like all was possible. She deserved it all: the moon, the stars and beyond. She'd saved my life. My beautiful woman - she was God in the flesh.

GOD IS A WOMAN

NINE MONTHS LATER

Dear Diary,

Los Angeles is a complete culture shock. The people are far more superficial and everywhere is one big fuck party. I have yet to land my first major writing gig. Thus far, I've only written a few scripts for low budget pornographic films. This place isn't for the weak-hearted. It will chew your confidence away day by day. On the bright side, my career as a spoken word artist has been making incredible strides. I tour four days a week and make five hundred dollars a show. There's a lot of temptation to do wrong on the road. A lot of beautiful women have fallen in love with my words and are willing to open their legs for me. Being faithful is hard and being sober is harder. Free drugs are everywhere I go: coke, shrooms, acid, heroine, you name it and it's there.

I see a shrink twice a week, now. Tough skin is needed to survive in LA. You may hear a million times no before getting your first yes. And at this point, I'm at 'no' number five thousand eight hundred and seventy-seven, and yes, I've counted. It's easy to lose your way, but I have my rock to keep me grounded.

I often find myself getting homesick. I miss the simplicity of my home city versus the fast-paced high life of Hollywood.

Being a good father to my baby girl, Sasha, is my number one priority, but I'm afraid I might find a way to screw up. Being a parent is an intense responsibility, but it is the one thing I must do right. I can't fail by her. I can't fail her mother, either.

Poor Mariana. She won't be able to see her baby girl grow up. She passed away soon after giving birth. At least Sasha has an angel for life. Since Mariana's untimely death, Iris has become my daughter's maternal figure. I'd always known she would be a great mother.

Overall, California is like living in a dream, and I never want to wake up. We live in a subtle two-bedroom apartment a few miles away from UCLA and life is good.... for now.

THE END

GOD IS A WOMAN

CONNECT WITH THE AUTHOR

Twitter: @MichaelTavon

Instagram: ByMichaelTavon

GOD IS A WOMAN

WORD FROM THE AUTHOR

From the bottom of my heart, thank you all for reading God is a Woman. If you enjoyed the story, please leave a favorable review on Goodreads or your favorite online retailer or tell a friend. Word of mouth is everything.

WORD FROM THE AUTHOR

From the bottom of my heart, thank you all for reading God is a Woman. If you enjoyed the story, please leave a favorable review on Goodreads or your favorite online retailer or tell a friend. Word of mouth is everything.

Made in the USA
San Bernardino, CA
10 July 2018